YOU, ME, AND THE VOODOO QUEEN

A MALVEAUX CURSE MYSTERY (BOOK 2)

G.A. CHASE

BAYOU MOON PRESS, LLC

Copyright © 2017 by G.A. Chase

First Edition 2017

Cover Art by Janet Holmes

Editing by Red Adept

ISBN eBook: 978-1-940299-38-9

ISBN Print: 978-1-940299-42-6

This book is a work of fiction. Names, characters, places, and incidents are products of the author's imagination or are used fictitiously. Any resemblance to actual events, locals, business establishments, or persons, living or dead, are entirely coincidental.

Bayou Moon Press, LLC

YOU, ME, AND THE VOODOO QUEEN

Kendell Summer just can't catch a break. All she wants is one good passionate kiss from her paranormal partner, Myles, but in the midst of their embrace, she hears a distress message coming from a passing paddle wheeler. Her band, Polly Urethane and the Strippers, is in trouble. Once again, she must drop everything and rush to the rescue while relying on Myles to have her back.

Unfortunately, the events that unfold while she's saving her friends only plunge her deeper into the dreaded Malveaux curse and threaten Myles with a fate worse than death. Kendell will need everyone she trusts, including her loyal dog, Cheesecake, to help her save his soul.

*M*yles only dimly noticed the light breeze off the Mississippi River and the joyous sounds of children headed to the Audubon Aquarium. Everything but Kendell faded to inconsequential background detail.

He held her tight in his arms. Her mouth tasted of the fresh strawberries and whipped cream they'd shared at the small outdoor café. Six months of dealing with the Malveaux curse, the fucking pipe tool, and the powerful Laroque family were finally in their past. They could love each other without reservation. She was his. Having confessed her love, she'd broken down the barrier they'd both maintained during their shared mission. Every part of her small, firm body pressed so hard against him he wondered how their clothing managed to separate them. Even her dog, Cheesecake, had them wrapped together in her leash. Life was good.

"Shit! I have to go." Kendell broke free of his embrace,

untangled herself from the dog's lead, and started running down the wharf.

"Kendell! What the hell?" He started chasing her down the old wooden planks, trying to keep hold of Cheesecake's tether.

As she ran, she shed her heavy peacoat. "Take care of Cheesecake! You're my salvation! The band needs my help. My girls are in trouble. I love you!"

In disbelief, he watched his friend jump from a gangway onto the passing paddle-wheeler steamboat. With the leash of her elderly overweight dog in his hand, he had no way of following her. As the boat pulled out into the Mississippi river, he heard the refrain of ABBA's "SOS" from the calliope. In the playful sounds of the carnival-like steam-powered organ, he could make out the hard-driving beat of Lynn Seed at the keyboard. Why Kendell's band, Polly Urethane and the Strippers, would be in trouble aboard the tourist boat was a mystery. But as he watched the ship churning up water, he knew there must be a problem. By tradition, music from the calliope only played while the ship was in port, not when it was underway.

He looked down at the pup, who was barking her fool head off at the receding boat. "It's okay, girl. We'll get her back." But without knowing what new danger Kendell had just jumped into, he struggled with where to turn next. The shaggy Lhasa apso might not be his most helpful ally, but she would be the fiercest.

As the steamship headed toward the big, easy bend of the river, he knew who would be his closest support—provided Professor Yates's psychometry research laboratory hadn't fallen off the rotting pilings into the river. Retrieving Kendell's coat, Myles found her keys in the pocket. Unfortunately, he also found her cell phone. Contacting her would be impossible.

He threw her coat over his shoulder and bent down to look the dog in the eyes. "I know you don't like being picked up by anyone other than Kendell. I'd just like to remind you that I did help rescue you. You're going to have to trust me just a little bit."

As he wrapped his arms around the dog's thick, curly coat, she began her low-pitched growl of disapproval.

"We don't have time for this, girl." Before she could revert to her wolf-ancestor persona, he whisked her up in his arms and headed for the bright-yellow scooter Kendell had parked near the restaurant. The dog continued to growl, but increasingly, Myles suspected that was more from the discomfort of his running than her anger at being so unceremoniously manhandled. "I'll drop you off at home first. You'll be relaxing in the sun in no time. Just work with me for a little while, then I'll go do what I can for Kendell."

KENDELL LAUNCHED herself off the wooden pier and stretched out her arms to grasp the brass railing of the passing riverboat. The water below her kicked up spray as the ship turned away from the levee. She scampered to find a foothold against the slippery steel hull. In her short spring dress, she felt all too vulnerable as the twenty-five-foot red paddle wheel tossed gallons of water over her head. At least she was wearing her tennis shoes. *I didn't dress for this kind of action.* Not that she could have anticipated the uncomfortable lunch where she introduced her mother to Myles progressing to a passionate display of affection followed by a rescue attempt. How was a girl supposed to dress for an afternoon like that?

Her band had been invited on the afternoon cruise by their fellow performers at the Scratchy Dog—a group called the Mutants at Table Nine. Of course, she'd declined. Even if she hadn't had a date with Myles and her mother, hanging out with a group of nerdy guys could too easily be interpreted as her being available. Their relationship was complicated enough.

She squirmed under the lower railing and onto the mercifully horizontal deck. She was soaked to the bone, but she'd made it aboard. As she lay there wondering what her first move should be, a shadow passed over her closed eyes. The hand that clasped over her mouth caused her to struggle but only until she saw it was Lynn Seed, who motioned for her to stay quiet.

Lynn, whom Kendell usually saw hiding behind her keyboards on stage, pointed toward the engine room. "We need to get out of sight. I'll explain everything once we're safe."

Kendell's ears hurt from the noise of the boilers, engines, and paddle wheel being driven by the monstrous connecting shafts. She searched the small room filled with menacing machinery. Somewhere, there had to be people operating the antique equipment. To her surprise, there was no one sitting at the bank of gauges and levers.

Lynn pointed toward the narrow hallway that led to the front of the ship. "He's working on the boilers. We can sneak through the workers' passage to the office upstairs. We should be safe there for a little while. They've only got the one guy working down here, so he's being kept pretty busy."

The nicely preserved engine room had signs warning tourists to keep their hands away from the equipment. The condition of the paint-chipped steel staircase and grungy office, however, contrasted sharply with the well-kept antique machinery in the next room. Kendell nearly bolted for the stairs on seeing the back of a tall, lanky redheaded dude rummaging through the ship's plans in the small office.

Lynn pushed Kendell through the oblong opening. "Don't worry. That's Lars. He plays keyboards for the Mutants at Table Nine."

The room barely accommodated all three of them. It felt even more cramped as Lynn pulled the hatch closed behind her.

Kendell would have worried about the water that dripped off her giving away their location if the whole deck weren't already covered in puddles. "Maybe you'd better tell me what's going on."

"I don't know. While everyone was having lunch, Lars and I snuck away to check out the boat." The way Lynn blushed left Kendell assuming their search had mostly to do with finding a quiet place to make out. "We heard a commotion from the dining room. When we peeked back in, we saw everyone tied to chairs and some heavy thug with a gun. That's when we hustled back up top and started playing for help on the calliope. I knew you were close by and would figure out my desperate plea."

Lars never did talk much, and when he did, he seldom made eye contact. Other than his lanky build and expertise on the keyboards, Kendell had no idea what Lynn saw in him.

"It's our fault," Lars said. "The guy said he was a fan. He'd heard the joint jam session and wanted to show his gratitude."

People who couldn't adequately express themselves bugged Kendell no end. "What are you talking about?"

His look of exasperation didn't help his cause. "He gave us the tickets."

Kendell turned back to Lynn. "Did you recognize anyone during the cruise?"

But apparently Lars wasn't finished. "What did I just say? The guy with the gun was the dude who gave us the tickets."

"He didn't happen to give you his name, did he?" Kendell considered slapping the answer out of his mouth.

"Stone, Boulder, something. I don't remember."

She began to wonder how much pot smoking had been going on. The guy was clearly high.

Lynn turned to him. "Did it sound like rock? Laroque maybe?"

"Sounds right. I didn't hear him very well. You know how it is after a gig."

Kendell closed her eyes at her own stupidity. Abducting the band was just a way for the powerful family to get their hands on her. But which faction of the recipients of the baron Malveaux's curse was to blame?

The options were almost too complex for her to pin down. The powerful members who were making a play for national office would want her for protection against the curse. They might even think it possible she could break the spell. Those trying to unseat the leading edge of the dynasty, however, would be looking to her to carry out the evil originally commissioned by her forefather. Then there were those like Lance, who only wanted his fair share of the family's prestige and wasn't above causing a bit of fuss to ensure he was heard.

"They're not going to hurt anyone," Kendell said. "Bad press is one thing that family can't stomach. They've made the first move, but they don't know I'm on board."

Lynn pointed at the ship's diagram. "There are four assholes holding our friends here in the dining hall. We only saw the one guy running the engines and the captain up top on the bridge. I don't think either of them is in on the kidnapping as the captain let me play the calliope. He could have turned us in. So what's our move?"

Kendell didn't like what she was thinking, but she didn't see a choice. "I know it's asking a lot. I need you two to allow yourselves to be captured. They'll keep searching the boat until they find you. Once you're back with the bands, you can let them know I'm working on their rescue. We need to find out what these guys are up to. They can't keep y'all on this boat forever, so I'm guessing they've got a destination downriver for you."

Lars's eyes were clearing from their fog as he got into the intrigue. "Then you'll go get the cops?"

If only it were that easy. Kendell still didn't know if Chief of Police Gerald Laroque was an honest cop or keeping all opposition to the family in check. After all, New Orleans wasn't known for its upstanding law enforcement. "Once I know where they're holding you, I'll find Myles. We have some allies the Laroque family doesn't know about as well as some other potential items from the baron that might prove useful as bargaining chips." But would retrieving more cursed items play right into the hands of those looking to capitalize on the family's dark past? Kendell knew she'd never needed Myles's help more.

She didn't want to leave her friends. Having others around provided a small sense of safety, but she needed the kidnappers to feel they had control so they would start discussing their plans. All she had to do was find a hiding place somewhere within listening distance to where they would be conducting their private meeting. *Right, that should be simple.*

Before she could locate a suitable location, she needed to be sure no one else would be prowling the decks. That meant the two lovers would need to be found first. Kendell squeezed on top of the life-preserver cabinet that ran along the passageway. Her small body was easily hidden against the bulkhead, but just to be sure, she peeked over the edge. Lynn gave her a thumbs-up before returning to her boyfriend in the engineer's office.

Waiting for Lynn and Lars to be discovered was agony. How could the search party be so dense? Of course, the couple had snuck off to make out. A small office, pantry, or alcove would make the most sense. As she heard the two men poking around the ship's bilge, she wondered if they thought the band members were international spies and not lusty youths.

The conversation with the haggard engineer came across loud and clear once he shut down the engines. "This isn't how things are done on a steamboat. These engines are from the 1920s. You don't just push a button and start them up. And without propulsion, we could drift into a sandbar. The captain's going to hear about this."

"You can have control back as soon as we've finished our search. I'm not losing a hand down here. Haven't you heard of safety equipment?"

The ship worker wasn't backing down. Kendell added him to the small list of people who might be willing to help. "Look, Bubba, get your hands off my equipment or grab a life vest. Because if you don't let me restart these engines, you're going over the edge one way or another."

"For a scrawny fellow, you've got a lot of grit. We'll be done in a couple of minutes. There are two kids hiding somewhere on this ship. Once we're done down here, you won't have to worry about us again."

Hatches banged as they were opened and shut, and tools hammered against metal as if someone were trying to drive a rat out of its hole. Kendell was glad she hadn't chosen that area for hiding. She squeezed even deeper into the gap between the cabinet and the ceiling. With every passageway lined with ducts and conduits, hopefully she'd be as unnoticed as the heavily painted pipes and valves.

A loud blast from the ship's steam whistle preceded the clamor of the engines starting back up. The sound of heavy boots on the metal stairs made Kendell hold her breath. "One deck down, two to go. I can't believe they'd be so stupid as to hide in an office, but the boss says to check everything."

The screeching of the hatch opening was drowned out by Lynn's scream. "Close the door, pervert! Can't you see we're busy in here?"

"Put your pants on. We're not here for the peep show. You two need to join the others on the main deck."

The footsteps on the metal passageway below Kendell receded. From somewhere down the hallway, a hatch opened then closed again. She checked her vintage Swiss army watch. With her heart beating so fast she could feel the pulsing in her fingers, she was tempted to jump down and sneak forward, but she needed to be sure they wouldn't come back and continue the search just to be thorough. As the minutes ticked by, she resisted the urge to hum a tune to calm her nerves. Being completely quiet for five minutes didn't come naturally to her.

The instant the second hand crossed twelve for the fifth time, she began working her way out of the tight space. Her soggy dress caught on the sharp edge of a metal support, tearing the hem. As quietly as possible, she lowered herself down to the deck. All the effort she'd put into looking as cute as possible for Myles while still not giving away her romantic interest to her mother seemed a distant memory. She looked at the rags that had been the dress she'd taken so long to choose. *I knew I should have stuck with jeans.*

Instead of heading in the direction the thugs had taken her friends, Kendell snuck down the stairs back to the engine room. The lure of hearing what the kidnappers had in mind had to be balanced against her need to remain undetected. With any luck, the engineer would still be busy getting the massive paddle wheel back up to speed.

The small number of people aboard worked in her favor. Everyone would have to be inside, guarding her friends. Outside, she had more options. Fore and aft staircases extended to all three levels of the ship. The breeze blew her wet dress against her body, making her feel even more exposed. Desperately, she wished Myles were there to help, but she was also grateful for having him on shore as her backup plan.

From the deck, she could see they'd steamed far downstream. The historic houses and wharfs of New Orleans had given way to bayous, oil refineries, and fishing villages. People out here were wary of strangers and kept to themselves. They weren't the type to offer help, even to a drenched young woman. If she or the bands were to escape, they'd likely be killed by alligators—or worse. She lifted the cover off a lifeboat and slipped inside. It might not be the cleverest of hiding places, but so long as no one was searching for her, it would be fairly versatile.

After what she estimated to be an hour out of New Orleans, the steamship gave a small toot of its whistle and slowed to a gentle paddle. Lifting the cover a couple of inches, Kendell saw a dock barely large enough to accommodate the tourist ship. As they nudged alongside it, she wondered why the gentle impact didn't crumple the rotting pilings.

She ducked back deep into the lifeboat as she heard voices from the deck above. "We've got a nice little warehouse for you folks. During the season, alligator hunters use it for selling their catch. Some of those gators linger around when they know it's safe, so it'd be best if you didn't try to escape."

She recognized Polly's voice of defiance. "How long do you intend to keep us as prisoners?"

"Not a moment longer than necessary. Once your friend does what we want, we'll provide you a nice dinner cruise home. Just pray she doesn't try anything stupid. I'd hate to have to hurt one of you to teach her a lesson."

2

*M*yles stood out front of the tattered warehouse, staring downriver. Somewhere around the bend, Kendell was facing danger alone. Her telling him she loved him only compounded his frustration at not being with her.

"What's up?"

Myles turned to see Professor Yates standing at the entrance of his improvised laboratory. As always, he looked as though he'd just woken up from a nap.

"Kendell's in danger, and I need your help." He proceeded to relay what little he knew.

"Why me?"

"You may be one of the only people in New Orleans who accepts my powers of psychometry. You also know better than anyone about Kendell's connection to the Malveaux curse."

The man wore the outfit he used to con tourists into psychic readings in the Quarter. It made him resemble a steampunk version of Dracula. He used his fingers to comb his gray hair away from his eyes. "You think this has something to do with the curse?"

"How could it not? Someone went to a lot of work and spent a sizable amount of money getting the band onto the riverboat. I've heard them play. They're fun but not worth that much effort. I can't come up with another explanation of why they would have been kidnapped other than to influence Kendell."

The lab that occupied the run-down office wasn't Myles's idea of welcoming, but the fact that the professor hadn't invited him in was confusing. Voodoo and curses weren't topics to discuss out in the open. "Well, we can't chase after them. If you're right, whoever's behind this will probably be on the lookout for another of the baron's old possessions. There's still a few hours until dusk, which is when business really picks up for me. I think it's time we had a longer talk with Madam de Galpion."

Though Myles had questions for the proprietor of Scratch and Sniff perfumery, he wasn't sure more talking was going to help Kendell. "Do you think she can help?"

"We kept some information from you two the last time you were in her shop. Partly, that was for your protection, but if the Laroque family is intent on using Kendell, it would be better if you had the full story."

Myles turned to look downriver. "Okay, but I don't want to spend all day talking. Kendell needs help now."

The sometime professor snatched his top hat from a

skull near the door. "Until we hear from her or are contacted by the kidnappers about what they want, there's not much we can do. I promise you'll find what Madam de Galpion says enlightening."

Though it was only a half-mile walk from the wharf in the Bywater to the creepy old house in the French Quarter, Myles felt every step took him farther away from helping his friend. However, he couldn't come up with an alternative plan of action. No matter how many times he played out who would be behind their latest misfortune, and why, all he could see was the dreaded facial features that distinguished the Laroques—the most direct descendants of the baron Malveaux.

Madam de Galpion didn't look any more awake than the professor had. Her nearly black eyes glared first at Myles and then at the professor. "If you insist on continually waking me up at this ungodly hour, I'm going to have to change my shop hours."

The professor didn't wait for an invitation to enter. "Four in the afternoon is hardly ungodly."

"It is when I don't open until nine at night. Not many strippers are out shopping for perfume in the afternoon. This must be important."

At least the shop didn't reek of incense as it had on Myles's last visit.

Professor Yates closed the door after Myles. "I'm afraid it is, Delphine. Our Miss Summer has gotten herself involved in another intrigue. If we're to save her, Myles is going to have to know the truth."

Madam de Galpion drew the lightweight fabric of the

Haitian wrap tight around her body. "That is unfortunate."

Myles had suspected the two knew more than they'd let on. Maybe if they'd been more forthcoming earlier, Kendell wouldn't be in trouble now. "I'd really like to keep this short if we can. She needs my help."

"Impatient as always, *mon cher*. Unfortunately, mine is not a short story. I too have a role to play in the Malveaux saga. My ancestor was the voodoo queen who cast the curse —Marie Laveau."

In spite of his need for action, Myles took a seat on the rickety wooden chair in front of the chemical-stained and burned table. "I'd always heard you were from Haiti."

"After Marie's fame, her daughters took up the business, but they were more interested in profits than reverence. My foremother moved back to our ancestral home to pursue voodoo in its pure form rather than be corrupted by greed. Haiti, however, is not a pleasant place to live. My mother brought me to New Orleans when I was a small child."

Myles searched for the creole features of the woman's face. Though her skin was blacker than that of any woman he'd seen, the telltale high cheekbones and aristocratic long neck spoke of a mixture of ancestral heritages. "But if you were removed from Madam Laveau's family, what would you know of her curses?"

"You've worked in the Quarter long enough to realize that most voodoo shops are little more than shadows of the true religion. My relatives had no idea what they had in their back rooms. Mother was able to gather Marie Laveau's possessions from her cousins with little effort. Mostly, she focused on anything Marie wrote. That turned out to be quite a lot."

Myles wondered how much of that effort was conventional and how much involved the dark arts, but it seemed impolite to ask. "Do you have her journals?"

Madam de Galpion pulled out a ring of keys from her desk and selected an old, rusty skeleton key. "I have more than that. Come with me to the back library."

He'd seen her workroom before, but he'd had no idea that behind the glass display case filled with totems was a door covered in Xs and foreign writing. He squeezed behind the floor-to-ceiling display to join her in the long walk-in closet lined with bookshelves. "What is this place?"

"These are all of the curses that have been cast by my family over the last two hundred years. Most of the recent folders are filled with fake incantations. I keep them categorized in case someone comes after one of us for misrepresenting our abilities. Of course, there is also the possibility that one of my cousins might stumble across a useful combination of babblings." She reached for a leather-bound journal that had dozens of companions along the back wall. "Marie was meticulous at recording as much information as possible—the backgrounds of both the one commissioning the curse and the person under the spell, potential side effects, results, and strange cryptic sayings that I've been unable to decipher."

Myles stared in wonder at all of the paper folders, journals, and heavily bound textbooks. "And she recorded what happened to Kendell's family?"

Madam de Galpion motioned him to a worn red-leather

reading chair opposite her ornately carved wooden throne inside her mystical library. "It's all here. Kendell Summer's forefather was Louis Broussard. He'd borrowed heavily from the bank for some agricultural experiment he was conducting on the Westbank of New Orleans. As that endeavor failed, he deeded more and more of the land to the bank as payment."

Myles knew enough of the history to know who sat in the head office at the time. "In other words, he deeded it to the baron Malveaux."

"Precisely. But as Mr. Broussard sold off his prime land first, eventually he was left with only swamp—not exactly the type of property the baron wanted for his new housing community. Instead of accepting the deed as payment, the banker demanded Mr. Broussard's wife and children to be used as indentured servants. The women were used in the baron's brothels, and the son was sent to work the docks."

Kendell had relayed much of the same information after her visit with her mother, but Madam de Galpion's version was less discreet.

"They became prostitutes?" Myles asked.

"Yes. Mr. Broussard, being a man of New Orleans, knew exactly what his family would be forced into. The baron had a preference for young, innocent girls. He would often keep a daughter of one of his indebted customers as his personal concubine for months before turning her over to one of his establishments."

Myles looked at the journal, but it didn't appear to be written in English. "Marie Laveau wrote all that down?"

"To cast a spell, she often spent entire nights with a

customer to get the full story. After leaving the bank, Louis Broussard spent the last of his pocket money on alcohol instead of using it for the ferry ride home. Marie found him nearly passed out on her front steps. He traded the deed to his remaining property for the curse."

Though Myles still worried about what Kendell was up to, the story of her family began to make more sense. "What exactly was the curse?"

"Though Marie was already legendary in New Orleans, so was the baron. She couldn't curse him directly without unwanted ramifications from the city's elite. Cursing his offspring was also problematic. Many of them, like Miss Summer's ancestor, were the result of unions with women who'd been kept as the socially acceptable version of white slaves." Madam de Galpion grew quiet as she read the journal.

Myles had done enough investigation with Kendell to know it was the baron's legitimate son who carried the heaviest burden for his father's actions. "We found out that his legitimate daughter, Serephine, was the first to fall under the curse, but his son seems to have taken it on himself to protect the family to the best of his abilities."

Madam de Galpion nodded as she continued to study the writings. "That would make sense. Marie cursed the items in the baron's immediate possession. Those would be things he regularly carried with him. But the curse would only affect those of the Laurette-Malveaux union—in other words, his legitimate children with his only wife, Fleurentine Laurette."

"We've got a pretty good handle on who those people

became, the Laroques being the most notable family," Myles said.

She continued staring at the journal. "Being the illegitimate result of both Baron Malveaux and Louis Broussard, Kendell is the key to the curse. The objects are merely tools. She has the power to turn the curse."

"What does that mean?"

Madam de Galpion finally lifted her face from the pages. "With the correct key, a lock can be turned one way to seal a door or the other way to open it."

Myles began to experience the familiar frustration he had any time someone tried explaining something they didn't understand. "That's not terribly helpful."

"In her hands, one of the baron's cursed items could be especially dangerous to any member of the Laroque family. But she also has the ability to free anyone from that destiny. Marie left one other comment. It's not one I understand. 'Once unlocked, the door can be opened from either side.' I'll have to give that one some thought."

Myles noticed an envelope tucked into the pages of Marie's journal. "What happened to the deed to the property?"

Madam de Galpion pulled out the yellowed parchment from between the pages. "Even with Marie's fame, a free woman of color taking possession of so much land next to a white neighborhood would have put her in danger." She opened the papers to show the original deed carrying the name Louis Broussard. "I fear it's not worth anything more than historical value. After the War Between the States, the land was confiscated by the northern army."

It was a link to Kendell's past. "I'd be happy to buy it from you, provided it's not needed for your Marie Laveau collection of documents."

She rubbed the paper between her fingers and took a long sniff of the worn parchment. "It's part of Miss Summer's history. I'll trust you to return it to her. Marie lists in the ledger that payment for the curse was satisfactory even though she didn't claim the property. I'll warn you: she wouldn't have said such a thing out of the goodness of her heart. There's more depth to this curse than we know."

Professor Yates, who'd been silently filling the tight doorway like a spectral ghoul, spoke up. "Sounds like we're going to need another of the baron's artifacts if we're going up against the Laroques. Once a paranormal object is surrendered to Mr. Noire, it's almost never seen again. So it's pointless for you to return to the old World Trade Center for the pipe tool you two were playing with before."

The only alternative that Myles knew of wouldn't be much more helpful than Mr. Noire in his mostly empty building. "I know a place where more of the baron's old possessions could have ended up, but the nuns aren't fond of letting men into their compound."

Madam de Galpion returned the journal to the shelf. "Unfortunately, they're even less welcoming to a voodoo priestess. With your skills at reading an object's past human energy, you should be able to identify something under the curse. Once you have it in hand, bring it to me. Perhaps we can sneak a little surprise into the Laroques' plans."

∾

KENDELL STAYED as deep in the life raft as she could manage while still lifting the cover a sliver to see who returned to the riverboat. Only two hulking figures walked up the makeshift wood-plank gangway. That would leave two thugs watching over her friends. Two guarding seven wasn't bad odds, but as those two undoubtedly had guns, she hoped Polly wouldn't take it on herself to do something foolish.

She lowered the cover back in place and tried to envision the dynamics in the crude warehouse. What Polly lacked in musical ability she more than made up for in commanding presence. The girls would follow whatever half-baked plan she thought up. And it wasn't as if the Mutants at Table Nine would have anything to say. Like Lars, none of them looked to have gotten laid on a regular basis in their lives. The three guys cooped up with four women would be too hopped up on hormones to think clearly. Guys like that were putty in the hands of self-confident women. Hell, Polly could ask the trio to be half-naked male dancers for the act, and they'd agree.

For just a moment she wondered if any member of the all-male band thought he had a shot with her. None of them could stack up to Myles. *Poor foolish boys.*

As the steamship began churning up water, she checked her watch. So long as the ship travelled at a constant speed, she might be able to figure out the location of the warehouse by timing exactly how long it took to return to the French Quarter.

Once the footsteps had receded, she lifted the cover a smidge to look at the river. Beyond the bayou, she saw the upper deck of a freighter. That could only mean the paddle wheeler had taken one of the tributaries that led off the Mississippi. There couldn't be many such rivers that were large enough to accommodate the tourist vessel. As the steamship rounded a bend to rejoin the major river, she checked her watch again. *Fifteen minutes from warehouse to Mississippi.* She sang the words in her head to make sure she'd remember.

Out on the river, boredom was her biggest threat. With only two thugs and two people working the boat, she had plenty of opportunity to get out and sneak around the vessel. Time after time, she resisted the urge.

What do I know? Figuring out her resources might help with the wait. She could estimate where her friends were being held. That wasn't something the thugs would anticipate. Getting there and freeing them would be a challenge, but with only two guards, they probably wouldn't be keeping a close watch outside of the warehouse. With such a quiet tributary, they'd be listening for any boat that might come along rather than hanging out on the dock, getting eaten by mosquitoes.

She kept coming back to who was behind the abduction. The Laroques wanted to use her for some purpose, and though she prided herself on her mastery of the guitar, she had to believe they were after her for her connection to that fucking curse. *Just one day. Why the hell couldn't I have had just one full day with Myles to explore our love? Best not to think about it.* After six months of working together, he wasn't likely to lose his passion for her. She checked her watch again. Half an hour gone. They had to be about halfway home.

The smell of cigarettes made her lower the cover just before she heard the sound of footsteps on the deck above her.

"Not a bad outing. The boss will be happy."

"She's never happy. You'd better pray that little girl is able to perform her duty."

"Hey, don't turn this on me. If you had retrieved that pipe tool, we wouldn't be in this mess."

A cigarette butt landed on the canvas cover over her head.

"Like I was going to push my way through Big G's goons? Cops were all over that parade."

"Okay, I'll drop it. You did manage the death of that busybody reporter. That was a thing of beauty with all those witnesses swearing it was an accident. I'm just not crazy about kidnapping a bunch of kids. We'd better get back inside. If someone on one of those tugboats recognizes us, we'll be in deep shit."

"Please don't say shit. I can still smell that demon dog's crap in my sleep."

Though the dognapping of Cheesecake wasn't a night Kendell wanted to remember, she silently promised her dog a special treat for the lasting impression she'd made on her abductors.

As the grassy wetlands transitioned to wharfs and brick buildings, she breathed a little easier. Even with a segment of New Orleans's most powerful family stacked against her, civilization beat the bayou any day.

The ship would be docking soon. Her mind told her to follow the goons for as long as possible, but her heart told her to run to Myles as soon as she could safely get off the boat.

3

*A*s Myles stood in front of Our Lady of Mercy convent, he reconsidered waiting for Kendell to return. She'd had enough of a challenge getting through the gates the previous time they'd been there, and she was a woman. Without her, he doubted he had a chance. However, he had no way of knowing when or even if she'd be returning with the riverboat.

Summoning up his courage, he rang the bell. People walking along the street gave him suspicious glances as he waited. The convent, with its towering brick-and-plaster walls, presented as stern a look to the outside world as the nuns themselves. If it hadn't been for Kendell, he'd have skipped out before anyone made it to the front gate. But she was in trouble, and that meant he had to buck up. Minutes passed without any indication his request had been heard within. He stared up at the security cam as if to say, *I'm not leaving.*

The heavy eight-foot-tall wooden gate opened only wide enough for a nun's face, draped in a black habit, to peek out. "We're not open to the public."

"I'm aware of that. I'm a friend of Kendell Summer. She visited you recently. Lance Laroque vouched for her."

"I remember her. We let her in, but that one-time courtesy doesn't extend to her friends."

Myles knew that at any moment the woman might shut the door in his face. He didn't have long to make his plea. "She's in trouble. It has to do with what you two talked about. I'm not asking to come in, but it's vitally important that I get hold of the box that was left for Fleurentine Laurette-Malveaux on the death of her husband, the baron. You know what I'm talking about. I have a place where the items can be secured."

The woman's glare softened only slightly. "Have you considered that those people who inhabit the abandoned World Trade Center might not be your friends?"

From what Luther Noire had told him and Kendell about the founding of his organization, it shouldn't have come as a surprise that the reverend mother would know of him. Blessed items and holy relics remained with the church. Items of a darker paranormal nature typically ended up in his care. "You don't trust him?"

The door stayed open only a sliver. Myles considered that a major accomplishment. "That's a long story—one that goes back thousands of years. Like two foreign countries, we often have our differences."

"If you'd prefer, we can return the items once we're through with them. You know Kendell's connection to the past." He caught himself and just avoided using the word *curse*.

"And why should I trust you? If Miss Summer wants the objects, she should come here in person." The door began to close.

"I'm her boyfriend. I helped her with that last problem. She's in trouble. The Laroques have her." It was an overstatement of what he knew, but this might be his only chance with the nuns.

"As I explained to Miss Summer, our system of organization isn't the most up-to-date. Come back in the morning. I'll put one of my novices on it tonight." She closed the door without waiting for his reply.

Myles made a mental note to bring an offering to the church when he returned as a way of saying thank you.

～

KENDELL'S HEART beat faster once she spotted the open-air pavilion with its brightly colored flags that announced the riverboat's dock. Instead of heading in, however, the boat swung farther out into the shipping channel and continued upriver.

Tugboats and barges plied the industrial area of the Westbank. To her chagrin, the festively decorated steamship nosed into one of the open dry docks. Behind the heavy steel walls, the boat would be impossible to see from the Quarter. Myles would have no way of knowing where she was.

From the overhead crane, she heard a workman address the captain. "That was a long test cruise. I was considering sending a pilot boat out to find you."

The captain spoke over the boat's public address system. "Sorry for keeping you waiting. Got a little mixed-up past English Turn."

"The river only goes two ways. How did she perform?"

"Boiler number two still has a blocked port. And there's a leak somewhere around the engineer's office. The whole area was covered in water."

As the men talked, temporary gangways were set up from the dry dock to the ship. "Right. I'll look into it."

No mention had been made of the guests. Kendell assumed the captain had been bribed for the non-pleasure cruise. He and the engineer left the boat, but as the two thugs remained, she decided to stay as well. She figured either their departure would be noted by the dockworkers, or they were waiting for someone.

The late-afternoon shadows lengthened until only the tops of the tugboat conning towers remained lit by the sunset under the Crescent City Bridge. She was feeling a little claustrophobic, having spent hours in the small life raft. Her dress had dried, but the uncomfortable feeling and stench of the caked Mississippi river silt that permeated her damaged dress wasn't much better than being soaked. The lure of a hot bath, Cheesecake's snuggles, and a glass of wine with Myles made her look longingly across the river.

She heard the security guard make his rounds. The two thugs were still somewhere on the boat. Her watch illuminated the time as being 7:50. It had already been a long day. The last thing she wanted was to have to sleep in the uncomfortable raft. Once it was fully dark, she'd try to sneak out. Hopefully, the ferry would still be running so she could cross the river to her home and all she loved.

As she snuggled down into the hull to wait, however, a set of headlights hit the canvas cover. She stayed as silent as possible. Footsteps, a lot of them, made the metal gangway sound like Minerva Wax banging out a rhythm on her snare drum.

Peeking out of the cover, Kendell saw the party had chosen the ballroom next to her for their meeting. A middle-aged woman with short, well-styled gray hair and a commanding presence glared at the two thugs who'd returned from the kidnapping. "How could you miss her? Explain this to me."

"She didn't show up with the others. What were we to do? We still have her friends as hostages."

The woman paced the room. "She'll be waiting for our demands. Since she didn't go to the police when her dog was abducted, I think we can hope she won't this time either. Not that it would matter. Gerald might not be on our side, but he never could cross me, even when we were children."

As Kendell inspected the faces of those in charge, she noticed the distinctive long, straight noses and tight mouths. They were Laroques for sure.

A man who could have easily been the woman's grown son addressed her. "We could force her to do it. It's not like we're asking for her to murder someone. She didn't have a problem with the pipe tool."

The elder woman shook her head. "It would look too suspicious. Your thugs' use of that thing to kill Marilyn didn't do us any favors. That kind of short-term thinking could sink all our plans."

Kendell was surprised he didn't grumble some passive-aggressive answer or offer a lame excuse. Instead, he stood straight for the criticism. "It won't happen again. But now that we have found the girl and are intent on the Malveaux option, we can up our timeline."

"Only if we can keep it secret. The slow way involved far less risk."

One of the henchmen lit a cigarette and blew the smoke out the window at Kendell. "We can keep those kids for a week out in the bayou before we'll need to worry about restocking provisions. Every day is dicey, though. I've used the two guys who are guarding them before. They won't hesitate to resort to violence should anyone get any clever ideas."

The woman nodded at the piece of information. "We'll ask for a meeting. If she's smart, she'll come prepared. Don't underestimate that curse."

"We'll be ready."

Her look of frustration cowed the two heavyset men. "Don't be stupid. The meeting will be about negotiation, not force. The last thing I want is two football linemen ganging up on a waif of a girl. Just for once try to consider the optics."

Kendell studied the face of the woman's son. He had the

familiar cocky air she'd seen in Lance, but he kept his emotions better in check. "I'll handle it personally."

The woman's tone softened slightly. "She'll respond better to you. Politicians often have the ability to talk candy out of the hands of babies and a woman out of her clothes. Just be sure you know which one you're attempting. She might look like a little girl, but she's got more grit than your two thugs put together."

"You didn't send me to all those gentlemen's finishing-school retreats for nothing." His response had just the right overtones of indignation without sounding confrontational. Kendell had to admire how he managed to layer his emotions.

The woman's smile turned Kendell's heart cold. "Time to start reaping the dividends of my investment."

He grabbed his expensive suit coat from the banquet chair. "I think we've done what we can tonight. There's a bar next to the ferry terminal that serves a decent steak. I could use something to eat."

In a mild state of panic, Kendell watched the party leave. With them at the restaurant, there wouldn't be a way to get to the ferry unseen. Not that she had any money on her. And as the restaurant was the only establishment open that late, she couldn't risk sneaking in there to borrow the phone.

She stared down the long, well-lit levee path. People were pushing strollers and walking dogs. Maybe someone in the old neighborhood would take pity on her. It could be her best shot of getting home undetected.

She waited a full five minutes after hearing the last

indication of anyone in the dry-dock compound other than the guard. With the gates locked, she wouldn't be able to walk out as brazenly as her foes.

As silently as possible, she eased out of the lifeboat and down the deck to the paddle wheel that loomed overhead. Though only twenty feet from shore, she'd still have to swim the deep channel. No matter how warm New Orleans could be in spring, the Mississippi was always cold from the melting snow and ice that fed it up north. She lowered her legs off the boat and into the gently moving current. With a deep breath, she took the plunge into the unwelcoming, murky water. It only took a few minutes to reach the muddy shore, but she was once again completely soaked and cold.

She collapsed on the silty ground under the ferry terminal.

"A Mississippi mermaid. Don't see one of those every day."

Kendell turned to see a homeless man bundled up in an old sleeping bag and holding a fishing rod. Telling him what she'd been up to could too easily turn into just another way of being caught. The Laroques would be more than happy to throw a few dollars at the guy for the information.

"Just call me Ariel."

He set down the pole and pulled a filthy wool blanket out from his trash bag of possessions. "You must be freezing. Wrap yourself up in this. Once you feel up to walking, we can meet up with some friends. They'll have a fire going by now and hopefully a little food."

The mention of something to eat reminded her of how

long ago her lunch with Myles had been. It seemed like a lifetime had passed since then. But even with the blanket around her, she felt entirely too vulnerable. "I'll be okay on my own."

He unfolded his sleeping bag to show her he was missing an arm. "I'm not a threat. I'm also not a homeless vagrant. I'm a river rat."

"I've never heard that term before."

From deep in the covers, he pulled out a laptop computer. The tourist stickers indicated it had traveled the length of the Mississippi river. "There are whole cultures that live along the river that no one knows about. I'm trying to document what oral traditions still remain."

She was intrigued but cautious. The distinction between being a river rat and homeless sounded important to him. "Why tell me?"

"So you'll not think I'm some sexual predator or rogue out to steal your nonexistent money. My offer of help is genuine." He tossed her his wallet. "I was in the military. That's where I lost my arm. You can check my credentials."

She flipped through the worn-leather sachet. From a laminated army identification card, a much younger and cleaner face smiled out at her. "Sergeant Emile Whitmore."

He reached for the billfold. "No one's called me that for many years. Most people call me Whit."

She still wasn't sure she should trust him, but the cold and hunger were getting the better of her. It would be a long night on her own. "I suppose I am hungry."

He stood and started rounding up his meager possessions. "A girl like you doesn't end up down here if she has any other options. So I'm guessing you're running from someone. We'll keep to the rocks along the river. No one walking along the levee will see us. It's about a mile to the camp. Think you're up for it?"

Her legs nearly failed her as she tried to stand. "I'll be okay so long as we don't move too fast."

4

A light breeze rustled the leaves of the Cottonwood grove that bordered the river. Kendell could still make out the lights from the old neighborhood upriver, but no one ventured far enough down the levee to be heard up on the walking path.

She'd never given much thought to how the homeless eked out their survival. Though Whit had made it clear members of the small commune didn't consider themselves truly homeless, the difference appeared to be a matter of semantics more than economics.

The small bonfire quickly warmed her through her soaked dress. The blanket over her shoulders helped. Her shoes and shins were covered in drying silt. She did her best not to focus on how bad the combination of wet clothes, mud, and perspiration stank.

People in the small compound pitched in to prepare the simple meal. She thought she should help, but Whit made it clear to everyone that she was his guest. He handed her a blue-and-white-speckled enameled-metal cup. The smell of strong coffee was so enticing she breathed it in twice before taking a drink.

"I put a shot of rum in it to help warm you. If you'd rather have your coffee un-doctored, I can pour you another cup."

She had to stay sharp, but the soothing alcohol eased her shivering. "The rum's welcome in the first cup, but I think just this once."

"Understood."

An elderly woman in a torn lime-green housecoat brought over three plates. "Abe caught a river gar, and the community garden donated some vegetables. So it's seafood stew tonight."

Whit took the plates and handed one to Kendell. "Thank you, Mary. This is Ariel. She washed up under the ferry terminal."

The dented metal plate and crude surrounding contrasted with the well-prepared food. Kendell savored the traditional holy trinity of onions, bell peppers, and celery that made up the base of the stew. The way Whit had explained her presence in the camp made it sound like such occurrences happened all the time.

Mary sat in a lawn chair facing Kendell. She didn't blink her light-blue eyes for an uncomfortably long time. When she finally spoke, her flat tone made her sound as though she was in a trance. "A man jumps in the river to die, and a century later, his angelic daughter walks out the other side."

Whit took the metal coffeepot off the fire and freshened

Kendell's cup. "Mary is the camp's resident oracle. She lives on that razor's edge of sanity and prophecy. Even she'll tell you not to take her too seriously, but she's more often right than many here would like to admit. Sometimes it takes a while to figure that out, though."

Kendell stared back into the woman's eyes. "Do you mean Louis Broussard?"

The woman put her hand to her mouth as if she'd seen a ghost. She closed her eyes and regained her composure. "How much of the story do you know?"

Kendell wasn't ready to divulge her true identity. "I didn't realize there was a story."

Whit motioned toward his bag. "I told you I'm recording the oral histories out here. The story of Louis Broussard is one of the founding legends of this tribe. The ancestor who lost it all. They're not staying in this Cottonwood grove by chance. As the progenies of his son, Arvin, they claim this land. They have no legal documents, and every parcel of property on the other side of the levee is spoken for, so this is the only area where they're not harassed."

The woman again seemed lost in her trance. "But you are not from Arvin's line are you, my dear?"

Kendell didn't see any harm in divulging information from so long ago. "My family came from one of the daughters, Lilianna."

The woman nodded as if that somehow made sense to her. "The angel."

Whit pulled his computer out of his bag and started typing. "We've only covered the history of Arvin. Mary is the tribe's greatest resource on their history. I haven't heard the name Lilianna Broussard."

Kendell feared becoming known as the descendant of the patron saint of the homeless enclave. "What did you mean by calling her an angel?"

Mary talked about the past with familiarity as though she were discussing the tribe's events of the day. "*The* angel. She sacrificed herself for the rest of the family. I don't know what happened to her mother or older sister, but from the stories handed down from Arvin, it was his middle sister who freed the family. By agreeing to remain in captivity until death, she got their captor to agree to freeing the rest of her family."

If Lilianna had only been in her early teens and was older than her brother, Kendell assumed Arvin would have been barely a teenager—if that old. Indentured servitude to the baron might well have sounded like being a prisoner. If Arvin's story was retold down through the generations, she could see how it might not completely conform to the facts as she knew them. "What happened to Arvin?"

The small group of people crowded in around the fire to hear Mary tell the story of their ancestor. She suspected it was a tradition they all clung to as the binding force that made them a family.

"He received a small stipend and was dumped on this side of the river with only the clothes on his back."

A teenaged boy spoke up. "Wasn't it fifty dollars? That was a lot back then."

Mary turned toward the youth and smiled. "Very good memory, Hawk."

No one seemed to mind the interruption. As the story progressed, if someone felt Mary had left out some vital detail or had deviated from the traditional telling, they didn't hesitate to speak up. The narrative described how their ancestor had managed to survive on his own in the growing community that sought to drive him out. It meshed well with what Kendell had been told of the baron taking Louis's land as payment for his debts and building the residential neighborhood.

The story drifted on for much of the night. They wanted to hear about Lilianna, but each time the subject was brought up, Kendell managed to veer them back to talking about themselves. Before they had a chance to question her about washing up on the riverbank, she snuggled under the blanket and fell asleep next to the crackling fire.

KENDELL WAS up before the first rays of dawn. Her muscles ached from sleeping in the camp chair. Her skin itched from the dried clothes and mud that stuck to her like an unwelcome cast. Only her sense of smell seemed happy about greeting the day as the scent of strong coffee again filled the air.

"I won't ask you how you slept." Whit filled a couple of cups from the seemingly never-empty pot.

A cruise ship worked its way upriver just beyond the trees. "I need to get across the river, but I don't have any money or my phone."

"Don't worry about it. I've got a boat. We can set off as

soon as you're ready. Now that it's not pitch-black out there, it shouldn't be any trouble making the crossing."

She restrained her excitement. The camp had fed her, warmed her, and provided useful information about her family. But as the cruise ship cleared the bend, she saw the lights from the French Quarter. Home was only a short ride away. "You've been very kind to me, but I'm ready to go home."

Mary gave her a hug as Whit gathered his bag. "You are family here. I know we don't have much of anything, but family looks after family."

It was hard for Kendell to tell if the rest of the community felt the same way as they prepared for their day begging on the streets. The walk to the river's edge proved how badly her dress had suffered the day before. Even her sneakers would probably end up in the trash. Hopefully, this early in the morning, she could slink the couple of blocks from the wharf to her apartment unseen.

Whit started up the outboard engine on the dilapidated wooden skiff. "She's not much, but I can get her into these little marshes without running aground. It can get a little choppy out on the river, though. Best to sit down and hang on until we're past the ships' wakes."

After the previous day on the riverboat, Kendell would have been happy to keep as far from the Mississippi as possible. But with her friends in danger, she doubted that would be possible. Sucking up her courage, she chose to see the crossing as an adventure rather than a nightmare.

Whit must have sensed her discomfort, as he engaged her in conversation to distract her from the boat's rocking.

"That story of Louis Broussard that Mary told you last night isn't unique to this community. I've recorded similar tellings as far north as Baton Rouge."

"Do you get much deviation in the details?"

He swung the boat into the wake of the cruise ship, which helped steady the rocking motion. "I've heard he fell in the river drunk, committed suicide, or was tossed in by a mugger. The common thread, though, is he lost everything first. The homeless along the river see him as some kind of patron saint. Don't ask me why. That's one I'm still trying to decipher. I guess everyone likes to think there's some noble story about how they've come to be at the bottom of the socio-economic scale."

The engine on the small flat-bottomed boat revved up as Whit turned the nose back toward the wave crests. They were getting close. She pointed toward her building. "I live over there."

Unlike the Westbank, on this side of the river, Whit couldn't just dock his boat wherever he pleased. He slowed the engine and crept along the pilings of the wharf until he came up on a worn wooden ladder. "This might be the best I can do. If it doesn't feel stable, we can wander a little farther upriver."

The last thing she wanted was to have to walk the length of the French Quarter, or worse, dock next to the tour paddle wheelers. "I'm sure I can make this work."

"One last thing before you go. Mary's comment on you being family wasn't made lightly. Her little clan might not appear to have much influence, but among the homeless, they are well respected. No matter where you go—a dark alley, an abandoned home, anytime you feel in danger—know there will be people keeping an eye on you. The homeless are the invisible watchers. Very little happens that they don't know about."

She began to understand his attraction to societies made up of people who eked out a living. Those surviving on the economic edge looked out for each other. "You've been more than kind to me. I do have one last request. My friends are being held hostage in a broken-down warehouse. I have a rough idea of where. If you could locate them and tell them I'm doing what I can, that would help put my mind at rest."

"Consider it done. I'll even help with the rescue when the time comes. In return, however, I'd like to document your story. It would fit in nicely with the legend of Louis Broussard. I'll be across the river for another couple of weeks, so you'll know where to find me."

5

Though he was exhausted both mentally and physically, Myles simply couldn't fall asleep. The couch in Kendell's apartment was plenty comfortable, but his constant worry about her occupied every thought. He should be out there doing something. Cheesecake wasn't much help with her look of accusation from the ottoman.

"At least I had some idea of where you were after your abduction. If I had even a guess about Kendell's location, don't you think I'd be searching for her?" He simply didn't know where to start.

Not for the first time that night, he got off the couch and paced the small apartment. It'd been a long night of worrying, and that wasn't what he did best. At least when morning came, he could pick up the artifacts from the convent. Going through them would give him something to do. But if she didn't show up by noon, he swore—Chief of

Police Laroque be damned—he would file a missing person's report. Maybe he could get Lieutenant Cazenave to listen. He hadn't betrayed Myles and Kendell to the chief last time, and though he might not admit to the existence of curses, it was his job to investigate the paranormal.

Having a plan helped, though noon was still six hours away. He imagined the nuns would be up before dawn, but knocking on the door before first light seemed presumptuous.

Cheesecake leapt off the ottoman and bolted toward the door before Myles heard the key in the lock. The dog was howling and whining with such animation he could nearly make out the words she was trying to form.

He felt as if his heart were pulling him toward the door. As it opened, Cheesecake practically knocked Kendell back into the hallway. He'd never seen the old dog jump and dance with so much vigor.

Kendell bent down and picked up Cheesecake. "Oh, I love you too, girl. I'm sorry I made you worry."

The dog only received the bare minimum of greetings. Kendell carefully set Cheesecake back down and raced into Myles's arms. "Don't let go."

She was a mess. The stench of smoke, fish, and Mississippi mud made his eyes water. Dirt crumbled off her dress as they embraced. None of it mattered. She was in his arms where she belonged.

"You scared the shit out of me. I love you so much. You're not supposed to run off like that just before someone tells you they love you."

She sighed softly against his cheek. "I'm sorry. I have loads to tell you."

He didn't want to let her go. "Me too. But first, I've got to go pick up the baron Malveaux's trunk from Our Lady of Mercy convent."

She hugged him so tight his ribs hurt. "You read my mind. We need those objects. Give me fifteen minutes to shower and burn these clothes."

As he sat on the couch, waiting for Kendell, Cheesecake snuggled to his side. He couldn't tell if she thought he had something to do with Kendell's return or if she simply shared his relief.

The woman who eventually emerged from the bathroom resembled the Kendell he'd had lunch with just the previous day and not the mud-wrestling champion who'd walked in the door.

"I always suspected women could get dressed in a hurry when they wanted to."

Her girlish giggle made him want to hold her in his arms again. "Well, it doesn't take much makeup to impress the nuns. But once we get back from the convent, you can be sure I'll be spending a good hour in the tub before making myself properly presentable."

IT TOOK a couple of trips to haul the four trunks the handful of blocks from the convent to the apartment. They filled Kendell's small living room. Once the nuns had dug up

Fleurentine's possessions, they were all too happy to be rid of the stuff. If the old-fashioned luggage had been any heavier, she would have asked Myles to enlist one of his friends. After the day she'd had, she couldn't be expected to perform strenuous labor. But sharing the task with Myles meant she had him all to herself.

"Who knew she had so much stuff?"

Myles opened one of the boxes and poked around in the contents. "I only asked for the box from the baron Malveaux."

She stood in the middle of the room in her jeans, with her hands on her hips, surveying her new possessions. "I feel a bit like a forgotten niece who just inherited the family's junk."

"They must have misunderstood."

She doubted it. He could be a little gullible at times. She opened the crate nearest to her. "This one looks like just clothing." The old dresses might make for interesting costumes should the band want a different look, but other than that, she didn't see much use for the outfits.

"I'm not faring much better. For someone who was living the life of a nun, she sure had a lot of clothes and jewelry."

Just to be thorough, Kendell dug down through the dresses to the bottom of the box. "I would guess these things gave her comfort, or maybe she kept them as a warning against what lay beyond the convent walls."

He pulled out a sheet of yellowed paper from the top of the next box. "Looks like this is what we're after. It's a catalogue of the baron's possessions. This is going to take a while." He unwrapped a bundle of cloth to reveal a pair of glasses. "Whoever packed this stuff intended for it to be kept safe."

"Hopefully, that was out of reverence for the dead and not a fear of the cursed items building energy the way Mr. Noire described." The idea of so many objects infecting her, Myles, and Cheesecake all at once made her reconsider searching through the belongings. "Maybe we should do this at Madam de Galpion's. She seemed to know what she was doing."

"More than you might think. Speaking of which, I've got something for you that I retrieved from her shop. I can't imagine it's worth anything." He reached into his jacket, which lay over the arm of the couch, and produced the deed.

Kendell stared at the technical description, trying to envision how the landmarks matched up to what she knew. "She didn't happen to include a map, did she?"

"Sorry, that's all that was tucked into Marie Laveau's journal." He proceeded to tell her about his adventure in Scratch and Sniff's hidden closet of curses.

"By now, you'd think I'd be less surprised. I should have made the connection when she said her people had provided services to the Laroque family for generations. Clearly, that had nothing to do with her skills at whipping up perfumes."

Myles played with the glasses. "I'm not sure I trust her. She was awfully chummy with Lance Laroque last time we were over there."

Lance was an arrogant, self-entitled prick, but Kendell didn't fear him like she did so many others of the family. "We need someone who knows what they're doing. Between the two of us, we can identify which objects are cursed, but I don't know what to do with them after that. The dangerous faction of the Laroque family isn't going to sit around for long. They'll want to meet with me soon about my friends. Maybe I can sneak in some cursed objects. No bodyguard is going to deprive me of my reading glasses."

Myles nodded. "They'll be useful weapons should things go bad. Madam de Galpion indicated you could change the energy of the curse. Do you have any idea of what she was talking about?"

She reached for the glasses. The magnification of the lenses was so slight she was able to put them on without blurring her vision. "You were the one who talked to her."

He scanned the inventory sheet. "I guess we don't have much of an option. There must be two dozen things on this list I'd consider possibilities for the curse. Maybe she can help modify the energy so it only obeys you."

"I don't want to haul this whole collection over to her. Just in case she isn't on our side, pull out half of the objects to bring with us. I have to go to work if I have any hope of keeping my job." She absentmindedly folded the glasses and tossed them into Fleurentine's clothing-filled trunk. If nothing else, they'd make a cool addition to her Olympia Stain costume.

"Once I figure out what's cursed and what isn't, I'll stop by the coffee shop. I'm not ready to let you out of my sight for long." His wink made her feel warm deep inside.

Returning to work while her bandmates were still in danger felt like a cruel joke. But there was only so much she could do on her own. Constantly bothering Madam de Galpion during the day when she would normally be sleeping carried too much risk. They needed her on their side.

"You look like hell." Her manager, William, never was much for diplomacy.

"It was a long, hard day yesterday. I didn't get much sleep."

He also wasn't much for compassion. "Guy at the corner table has been asking for you since we opened. Don't make it a long conversation."

She repressed her snarky response. Jobs weren't hard to get in New Orleans, but William had been pretty forgiving of her tardiness. Late nights playing with Polly and the girls at the Scratchy Dog made for painful mornings serving coffee. She grabbed the carafe of freshly brewed dark roast and headed for the table.

As the man set down his paper, she nearly threw the coffee in his face. His Laroque features and unruly hair were unmistakable. She recognized him as the one being groomed for greatness from the night before. "What do you want?"

"We've taken seven of your friends as hostages. All we want are the baron's possessions. We'll exchange one item for each person."

She set the coffeepot on the table. "What if I can't find seven things? After all, you spent considerable time trying to find that pipe tool."

He wore his arrogance as casually as his off-center tie. "I'm not stupid, and you're a smart girl. You found one object. Where there's one, there's bound to be more. I'm sure you won't let your friends down."

If he knew about the convent, he wasn't going to admit it. Lance Laroque had supplied the lead to the nuns and Fleurentine Laurette-Malveaux's chests. Lincoln's ignorance meant either Lance really wasn't working for that side of his family, or they were intent on keeping his cover story intact.

"How long do I have?" Kendell asked.

He folded up his paper and made to leave. "I'll stop by each morning to check on your progress. If you haven't located anything within a week, your friends will start suffering the consequences."

As he left, she again weighed the need for the job against the satisfaction of dumping two liters of hot coffee down his back. Discretion won out, but that was largely due to the pot's locking top.

She was still seething with anger when Myles strolled into the café. "What's eating you?"

"Damn. I hoped my emotions weren't that obvious. That guy from last night stopped by with their terms." As he sat at the table near the window, she wished she could join him, but one look at William, and she knew her conversation with Myles would have to be in short segments between serving other customers. "I have to get back to work. My boss is all over my ass today."

"Don't mind me. I'll just enjoy the show." His smile as he

checked out her bottom did little for her need to be responsible.

"Unless you want me to end up working at your bar as one of those cheap-hoe shot girls, you'd better stop distracting me." Even though she knew better, she couldn't help but give him a slight hip bump on her way back to the counter.

6

*M*adam de Galpion opened each cloth package with the care she might give a piece of priceless porcelain. As each was revealed, Kendell had the familiar disappointment she'd had as a young girl receiving underwear in her Christmas presents. Not one of the baron's things looked in any way out of the ordinary. An ink pen, a pocket watch with chain, a monogramed cufflink —on and on, the items revealed just looked like plain ordinary things her father might have on him. She knew that had been Marie Laveau's intention. Cursing such innocuous items would make them all the more dangerous. They wouldn't be kept safe under glass because of their historical significance. These were meant to be in everyday use.

Madam de Galpion sat behind the battered wooden table in the small closet filled with journals. "This is dangerous."

Kendell wondered why everyone felt the need to preface their actions with the warning. By that point, saying something was dangerous was like saying it was hot and humid in New Orleans. "We're pretty well versed in the curse by now."

"Getting hurt by one of these things is not my concern. Marie was a voodoo queen. At best, I'm a novice. To meddle with one of her curses is like trying to fix a Swiss watch that isn't broken."

Myles stood close to the door and away from the table. "You told me you could do it. What could go wrong?"

"That's one of the things that concerns me. I don't know. The last page of the curse refers to a missing journal. So it will be like me trying to fix that working watch without the full diagram of where everything goes and what it's supposed to do."

Kendell sat in the leather chair opposite Madam de Galpion. For the first time, the woman looked unsure of what she was doing.

"The segment of the Laroque family that wants to use the curse is sure to cover its tracks," Kendell said. "As near as we can tell, that's why Marilyn was murdered. She knew too much."

Madam de Galpion ran her fingers over the curse diary as if she were trying to placate her ancestor. "And you're even farther along in understanding their plans, which makes you more of a target."

"Not just us," Myles said.

His veiled warning only made the voodoo priestess shake her head. "They wouldn't dare come after me. Even though my skills are only rudimentary, Marie put in some protections for those following in her path. You don't see many voodoo queens meet with suspicious deaths."

Kendell was beginning to wish she still believed curses to be the stuff of fairy tales. "The Laroque family wants these things as payment for my friends' return. I don't want to see another *accidental* death like Marilyn Fontenot's. I just want these things to go back to being just things."

Madam de Galpion took Kendell's hand. "*Ma chère*, these objects will always be dangerous. The best I can do is make them more treacherous in your hands than in others'. You will have power over the items. As intended by Madam Laveau, they will be most dangerous against the baron's legitimate heirs, and only you will be able to activate the curse."

Myles's presence gave her comfort. "Can you explain what you mean by *balance*?"

"It's similar to the physics theorem that for every action there is an opposite and equal reaction. One of the reasons Marie took such care to investigate a client's history was to be sure her curses wouldn't backfire. The wrong that necessitated the spell couldn't be less damaging than the effects of the spell. In the case of Baron Malveaux, Marie believed the cumulative damage of the wronged parties whose families he'd forced into indentured servitude would more than balance out the generations of people who might be harmed by the curse."

"But having those who the curse was aimed at use it against their own family to gain power must confuse the balance," he said.

"True. And the curse is more powerful in the hands of a descendant of Louis Broussard to begin with. I worry about concentrating so much force."

Kendell had trouble envisioning all the people involved. "So I would be taking the place of everyone he wronged? That's a lot of responsibility."

"Hopefully, now you have a better idea of what you're asking of me."

Myles put his hands on Kendell's shoulders. "Yesterday, you said something about Kendell being the key that could turn the curse in either direction."

"Marie wrote in riddles and not always in English. My modifications would be based on her description of an heir to both the baron and Louis having the energy needed to manipulate the outcome. It's complicated and dangerous."

Kendell put the cufflink in the center of the table. "Then let's start with something small and see how it goes."

"One item is likely all we'll be able to handle each night. The energy required will drain us both."

It had been a busy thirty-six hours for Kendell. She'd chased after her friends, snuck around on the paddle wheeler, landed in the river, been rescued by a river rat, learned about her homeless relatives, retrieved the baron's objects from the convent, faced a member of the Laroque family, and had just received the news that she'd be in for an exhausting night modifying the curse. But she didn't see much choice. The kidnappers had given her a week to retrieve the items. Giving them up—as tempting as it was to save her friends—could turn loose a whole new brand of hell. If the Laroque family really was intent on gaining power through the use of the supernatural, who knew where their plan might lead? "One item at a time will only barely have them ready by the deadline."

"There's also the matter of payment. So far, our meetings have all been consultations. I give Cornelius Yates a lot of leeway in offering my opinions to his friends, but even I must earn a living."

Kendell couldn't imagine what type of payment she expected. "We're just service workers."

"You both have powers that interest me. I'll expect paranormal favors that I can call in from either of you at any time until I'm satisfied."

The undefined nature of what might be expected left Kendell hesitant, but what choice did she have? "Okay, but only if we can start tonight."

Madam de Galpion turned to Myles. "It would be best if you left the room."

From the way he grasped her shoulders, Kendell knew he wanted to object. Though she craved his presence, having him out of harm's way again seemed the smarter play. She looked up into his worried eyes. "I'll be okay."

"I'm not leaving the shop."

"You can man the sales desk. I'm sure my clientele will enjoy having a male presence." Madam de Galpion left out the cufflink but wrapped the remaining items in a metal-lined cloth similar to what Mr. Noire had used for the pipe tool. "Secured in the convent, these items wouldn't have absorbed much human energy, but now that they're back among the general population, they need better care."

~

WITH ONLY MADAM DE GALPION sharing the small sealed room, Kendell noticed the difference in human energy. The mutual longing between her and Myles was like two magnets dancing around each other, desperate to connect. Though he was in the next room, the rough-hewn door, exotic smells, and presence of the voodoo priestess had an isolating effect on her emotions. "How does this work?"

As the smoke from the incense started filling the room, the dark woman looked like little more than a shadow that swirled the air currents. "The one area in which I do excel over Marie is my command of smells. We'll start off filling the room with a fragrance signature similar to what she used. That will help us connect to the cufflink. Once we've established that connection, we'll be able to weave our souls into the curse from the item's perspective."

The trip back in time that Myles had taken her on with the pipe tool was an experience she would never forget. "So we'll watch Madam Laveau perform the curse? Will I see my forefather?" She tried to contain her excitement.

Madam de Galpion's black eyes penetrated the gray wisps from the candles. "Myles has taken you on such a journey?"

She feared she might have shared too much without meaning to. "He has remarkable skills, though he would tell you it's just his overactive imagination." The words floated out of her as if the dark woman had summoned the truth.

"I suppose I'll have to request such a journey as one of my payments. Tonight, however, we're not concerned with the cufflink itself. We'll be using it to move into the curse like a stepping stone we use to enter a river."

Kendell didn't like the sound of that. She'd felt that black wave when she experienced the pipe tool's history. "You're not worried that we'll be consumed by the curse's current?"

"Did you not hear me when I said this would be dangerous? The Malveaux curse will get seven attempts at claiming our souls. To effect the change we want, we'll need to bathe naked in its energy. Only as a participant in its force can we influence its direction. Hold my hands. We have a long night ahead of us."

Kendell knew what it was to get lost in a wonderful piece of music, to be whisked into an ethereal plane after intense sex, and even to be so captivated by her dog's eyes that she saw life as a beautiful sharing of souls. But as the aromas that filled the room took command of her sinuses, she experienced an overload of olfactory stimulations. Every other change of perspective on life had involved her remaining grounded in her existence. Madam de Galpion's chants in the darkness were like being pushed off a cliff.

Memories swirled around her. She grasped at the closest memory, the one Myles had recommended on their shared journey. A twelve-year-old girl buried her face in the snow-white and jet-black fur of a puppy to hide her tears of joy. The small dog licked the girl with such determination she wondered how her skin didn't prune up. But the girl was only someone Kendell used to be.

Madam de Galpion's black hand touched her shoulder and pulled her back into the swirling vortex. No words were exchanged, but Kendell knew she wouldn't be able to rely on that signpost back to her normal life. The voodoo priestess expected complete submission.

She experienced pure hatred distilled out of countless wrongs. Like small threads of razor-sharp fiberglass, the hatred sliced through every piece of living flesh it encountered. That was their black river, who she'd become. No person unfortunate enough to end up in the curse's stream could survive the piranha-like attack. But the river was wide, and her awareness only extended to the riffle of water next to her.

The smells changed, matching a bend in the river—scents she couldn't identify. But like putrid flesh, some things didn't require an explanation to be revolting. Somewhere far off in her awareness, her body was convulsing from the stimulants. If only she could struggle her way back to the memory of her and her dog. But a black shadow prevented her from turning in that direction.

We still have far to go. Though the words were not her own, she knew their truth.

A second series of aromas combated those of rotting flesh. The sickly-sweet, overbearing fragrance corresponded with a memory of an overweight woman wearing poorly applied lipstick, putting out a cigarette in a jelly donut. She didn't know the woman. Not that it mattered. The smell rolled the water, and her body, toward an upcoming narrowing of the river.

The long, fibrous blades fought with each other like salmon struggling upstream. They were all moving at breakneck speed toward the same constriction. She tried to slow her pace, but she had nothing to use as a break. She was the water that drove the action, and she was the threads of pure hatred. As the impenetrable rocks of scent forced her and the hatred together into one being, her awareness spread to every drop of the river. No one else would ever manage the waterway.

An overwhelming sense of power replaced her helplessness. As the water shot past the narrowing, she was free. No riverbed recaptured the water's direction. The dark energy was hers to do with as she chose.

Kendell returned to her body in a coughing, choking fit. She was on the floor. The large, heavy chair lay on its side. Vomit oozed around her head and into her hair. "This has not been a good week for my hygiene."

Madam de Galpion didn't look much better as she sat curled on the floor next to her. "I warned you this would take it out of both of us."

7

Kendell pulled her jacket tight around her body. She wasn't cold, but for the second time in twenty-four hours, she stank to high heaven and was covered in disgusting slime. "This wasn't how I envisioned starting our relationship."

Myles didn't even have his hand on her waist as they walked back to her apartment, not that she blamed him. "We've been through a lot worse than mud and vomit. But even in the shop, the smell from the back was overpowering."

She hadn't forgotten that he'd been in there. At some point, he must have hung the *closed* sign. No stripper would want that stench to permeate her tiny outfit. "Hopefully, the only thing you noticed was the smell."

He seemed to have trouble making eye contact. "I wish that were true. I nearly broke down the door at one point. You were screaming and cursing. The only thing I can equate it to was when Cheesecake had swallowed the pipe tool and we were trying to save her from the dognappers in the warehouse. Imagine giving words to her primal howls, and you'll get some idea of what I heard."

Kendell had never been shy about using expletives, but considering her condition on coming out of the trance, she could only imagine what she'd said. "You know that wasn't me, right? I don't even remember most of what happened. At least our trip into the pipe tool's history was filled with images. This was all blackness." She shook her head, trying to make sense out of what she'd experienced.

"That's what worries me. I thought Madam de Galpion was going to work on the cufflink, not on you."

She fished the small golden piece of jewelry from her pocket. It still just looked and felt like something she'd find on her father's dresser. "Something has changed. I just don't know what yet."

"Do you want me to hold on to the objects? When we were experimenting with my psychometric skills, it helped to not be around them all the time."

She handed over the cufflink. "You're not worried they will affect you?"

"Assuming Madam de Galpion did what she intended, only you would be able to use them against me." He turned the small item between his fingers. "I could try to read it, though. I'm kind of curious what it would reveal after the change."

Her stomach recoiled at the idea. "I'd rather you didn't. We're not playing anymore. I couldn't survive losing you to that black river."

"Fair enough." He pulled out a cloth bag and dropped the cufflink into it. The interior reflected the light as if it were lined with gold. "Madam de Galpion gave me this while you were cleaning up. She said it's probably not necessary now that you alone can activate the curse. I think she was looking for some way to ease my fears."

"Of me?" She asked the question before really thinking.

"Maybe. I get the impression we're in uncharted waters even for her."

While Kendell had feared Myles's reaction to the results of her latest adventure, Cheesecake's greeting as they entered the apartment left her heartbroken. The usual exuberance of seeing Kendell return home quickly changed to whimpering. The dog crawled on her stomach, whining, then backed away. On her second attempt at greeting Kendell, she raised her hind haunches and started to growl before once again slinking away.

After eleven years with Cheesecake, Kendell knew most of her moods. This one was a combination of fear for her human and self-protection against a perceived threat. Unfortunately, Kendell had triggered both reactions. She lay flat on the floor so only her face was presented to Cheesecake and slowly slinked forward. The action of getting down to the dog's level never failed to elicit the pup's love. Kendell breathed a little easier as Cheesecake crept up and started licking her face.

"It's okay, girl. I know you're worried about me. I've had a rough couple of days, but it's still me. I just need another shower. You'll see. Everything is going to be okay."

MYLES HADN'T SPENT SO much time couch surfing since the summer of his freshman year. Fortunately, Kendell's was one of the more comfortable sofas he'd encountered. After each session in the voodoo shop, she appeared so drained and beaten he simply couldn't leave her alone. But his main aim was to take care of her and keep her company. Though they'd kissed, moving the relationship to the bedroom when she was so vulnerable wasn't in his nature.

Cheesecake stared at him forlornly from the ottoman. At least she hadn't barked and carried on as she had on the first night, but he knew he wasn't the only one worried about Kendell's condition. "You're right. It's time I did something." Sitting by and watching weren't his strong points.

The smell of strong coffee had a way of enticing Kendell out of her bedroom. Even half-awake, with rumpled hair, and in her comfortable nightshirt, she was irresistible. If only they were in a time and place where he could act on those desires. "Cheesecake and I have been talking. We don't think you should go back to the voodoo parlor tonight."

"What choice do I have? They're going to hurt my friends. Even at this rate, we'll barely have enough time."

He'd hoped the idea of him and her dog being in agreement would brighten her mood. "The Laroques didn't worry too much about hiding their identities. That's unusual for a group trying to cover their tracks. Unless they've got some kind of a memory spell to make everyone forget, I think the Strippers and the Mutants are in more danger than we thought. It'd be awfully easy for the

Laroques to say our people wandered out into the bayou and got eaten by gators. It wouldn't be the first time someone had gotten lost out in those tributaries. Your friend the river rat should have found their camp by now. I want to go after them."

She brought her cup of steaming coffee to the couch and sat so close to him he had to resist the urge to reach out and touch her bare leg. "I've been so focused on getting these cursed objects modified I hadn't considered that we know the identities of the kidnappers. Even if we could rescue our friends, we'd still all be in danger."

Everyone was in danger, and he was proposing going up against armed thugs like some kind of stupid cartoon gang. So why was he having such a hard time resisting every section of her exposed skin? "You are bringing the curse together under your power. I don't like it, and neither does Cheesecake, but it does give us an edge. From what you said, it sounds like Chief of Police Laroque isn't part of their operation. I can't see him going against his own family, but once our friends are safe, we might be able to solicit his help or at least talk to Lieutenant Cazenave. We have allies."

She leaned down to face her dog directly. "I never wanted to make either of you worry. I love you."

Cheesecake quickly leaned forward to incessantly kiss her face.

Myles knew she wasn't going to like his next idea, but he'd had more than enough of her risking her neck. "I don't want you along for the rescue. It's not that I think you're too delicate or any BS like that. But you are pretty drained from your work with Madam de Galpion."

The way she sat up straight and stared at him with squinted eyes told him he was in for a fight. "No way. They're my friends, and I'm not putting you in danger without being there too. I love your desire to be my white knight, but we are not starting out our relationship with me as the weak girl and you as the strong man. Besides, unless you intend on taking a crash course on shooting a gun, I'm the only weapon we have."

He'd planned on a covert mission where violence wouldn't be needed, but she was right. He wasn't exactly the best in a fight. "What if they're watching you?" It was the last card in his hand of arguments.

"Then we're in deep shit. Any thoughts on how we go about turning ourselves into navy commandos?"

If the Laroques were keeping an eye on her beyond the daily morning meetings, they'd know about her sessions with Madam de Galpion, and he still couldn't be completely sure the voodoo priestess was on their side, and only their side. "First we need to see if Whit found their location. You said they weren't watching the river. As it's alligator mating season, I'm hoping they're also leaving the security of the bayou to the wildlife. We might be able to sneak in through the marshes if we can round up some people who know the area."

"I'll bet my family on that side would know some people. And thanks to you, I even know how we might be able to pay them."

～

SNEAKING across the river was easy enough. The Laroques didn't have anyone watching the ferry, or at least no recognizable member of the family. With the distinctive long, straight nose and tight, small mouth, anyone of that lineage was hard to miss. Not that they didn't have the money to hire whomever they liked.

Myles stopped Kendell from heading straight under the terminal the moment they disembarked. "I didn't notice anyone suspicious, but just to be sure, let's give it a minute to make sure everyone finds their cars without getting lost."

"You have no idea how hard I found it to take my time on my last outing." She sat on the cement bench as if they were waiting for a bus. "I noticed Whit's pole as we docked. Once the ferry pulls away, we shouldn't have any trouble finding him."

He knew they were putting a lot of faith in what the river rat might be able to do for them. Myles had his own resources, but utilizing any of them might attract attention. "You said he had a boat?"

"A river skiff. It's not much. I'm not sure how it would do in the bayou. I wish we had more of a plan."

He agreed, but saying so wasn't likely to give her confidence. "We're just on a scouting mission. I'd hate for Cheesecake to miss dinner."

"I asked my neighbor to check in on her, just in case."

The loud ship's horn preceded the rumbling of the engines that shook the cement bench. This was as alone as they were as likely to be. Only the security guard in the terminal, reading her romance novel, was left behind. "Let's do this thing."

He followed Kendell as she snuck around the side of the sculpture of Louis Armstrong like a drunk tourist looking for a quiet place to barf. The grass quickly gave way to sandy silt as the riverbank sloped down toward the water. He ducked behind the cement retaining wall that buttressed the small parking lot. In a matter of only a hundred feet, he'd gone from respectable urban dweller to the world of the underclass. She took his hand as they walked along the pilings that supported the terminal. "He's kind of disreputable looking, but he was kind to me."

I'll bet he was. Myles didn't think beautiful young women would often find their way to the river rat's daytime lair.

She turned toward a shadowy corner of the cement foundation. "Whit, is that you?"

"My Mississippi mermaid returns. I wondered when you'd show up. And you've brought protection this time?"

She hunkered down next to the pile of blankets. "It's not like that. He's my boyfriend." Myles's heart instantly felt like it was about to burst. She'd used the word so casually it sounded natural and obvious, but it was the first time he'd heard her confess their relationship to someone else. "Did you happen to make contact with our friends?"

The stack of brown wool blankets started separating. A short, dirty, muscular man in his thirties emerged. "I did. They're okay, or at least they were last night. Are we going after them?"

That was the real question. "We're a little light on a plan and resources."

"Then you're in luck. I assume Ariel told you I was in the military."

Kendell helped him gather his things. "It's Kendell. Kendell Summer. And this is Myles Garrison. I'm sorry I lied last time, but I didn't know you."

"No need to apologize. Are you still on the run, or can we take an easier path to the camp?"

Myles surveyed the path they'd taken. "I didn't see anyone following us, but we're no experts when it comes to surveillance."

"Right. Grab a blanket, and throw it over your shoulders. They stink a bit, but no one will bother looking you in the eyes if you appear homeless. We'll stick to the batture."

THE CAMP WAS SMALLER than Myles had imagined. There couldn't have been more than a dozen people milling around the fire and makeshift kitchen. As Kendell shed the mud-encrusted blanket, a matronly woman dropped her ladle into the pot and rushed up to embrace her. "My river angel."

Kendell pulled out of the embrace but kept her hand on the woman's waist. "Mary, this is my boyfriend, Myles. I'm afraid we need your help again. But before I ask, I have something for you." She pulled out the yellowed deed to the property. "I doubt it's enforceable, but it does prove your oral history."

The woman carefully unfolded the document. Tears filled her eyes. "At the very least, they won't be able to kick us out of our Cottonwood grove again. I won't ask you where you found it. That would only lessen the magic. We would have offered you our full support anyway, but with this, we're now in your debt."

"This deed belongs to you whether you can help or not. I need to rescue my friends, but I don't even know where to begin."

Whit began drawing in the dirt with a stick. "I located your friends at the edge of the bayou. A river approach would be too easily noticed, but I have a friend with an airboat that can get us over the water-hyacinth bogs. It's too noisy to get close to the warehouse, though, and it's not that great navigating the cypress grove that borders the river."

Mary inspected Whit's crude map. "We have relationships down there among the alligator hunters. They use flatboats. Some even stick to paddling them for the versatility."

Myles suspected Mary's connections might not bother with such mundane government restrictions as hunting tags. To pass quietly along the bayou often meant hiding more from people than wildlife. "So we use the airboat to get over the marshy section then switch to the flatboats to get close to the warehouse. How do we get our people out?"

Kendell started tapping out a beat with a stick against a rock by the fire's edge. "Can anyone in the camp do an imitation of a nightingale or some other bird that sings in the swamps at night?"

A boy not much into his teenage years let out a lovely whistling song. Myles wasn't much into birdcalls, but he'd have been hard pressed to imagine the sounds coming from anything but a bird.

Kendell looked intently at the boy and started tapping

out her beat while humming a phrase. The boy had the notes almost perfectly on his first try.

It took Myles a number of renditions before he remembered the song. "'Take a Chance on Me'? Seriously?"

"It needs to be an ABBA song as a response to Lynn's playing of 'SOS.' What do want me to use? 'Waterloo'?"

"No, you're right," Myles said. "That would be worse. Just promise me when this is all done you'll play me something to get the earworms out of my head."

With remarkable attention to detail, Whit drew a rendering of the warehouse raised on stilts. "If no one's looking, or your friends can create a distraction, we can sneak under the structure with the flatboats. There's a trapdoor used for hoisting the gators up out of the boats. It's our best access point."

Myles knew he'd be useless in a fight. "Then comes the hard part. How do we get our friends out? Even if we can open the trapdoor from outside, there's sure to be someone keeping an eye on them."

"Even if I had two arms, I swore off the use of guns when I left the army," Whit said. "Our best shot is to go late at night and hope one of the guards is sleeping. I'd suggest two boats. I'll take Myles in one. It'll be a surprise attack. Once everything is secure, Kendell and Hawk can come in and help transport everyone away."

Myles knew all too well what Kendell was playing with in her pocket. Two cursed items had been custom fit for her use. Fortunately, she kept her weapons a secret.

8

*E*ven with Mary sending her messengers downriver to deliver her request, Myles wondered if it wouldn't have been a better idea to wait a day or two. But the need to keep Kendell from enduring another night with Madam de Galpion, and their friends from spending another night in captivity, convinced him to proceed with the plan. Mary and Whit assured him that help would be forthcoming.

They made their first rendezvous as the last light faded from the cloud-covered sky. As Whit had promised, his friend waited at the river's edge. "We shouldn't have any trouble getting through the bayou so long as the rain holds off. We'll meet members from the Prejean clan at a summer hunting cabin I use for storing my gear."

Myles didn't have a chance to ask what that equipment might be as the roar of the eight-cylinder Chevy engine that powered the six-foot propeller drowned out even his contemplations. With one hand around Kendell's waist and the other holding tight to the side of the seat, he held on for dear life as the boat swung from side to side through the thickening mat of plant life. In daylight, and without the dangerous mission, the trip might have been a lot of fun. But in the pitch-black night with only the small light at the front of the boat, he feared he was about to lose his dinner —or become someone else's.

He tried focusing on the small beam of light ahead of the craft. Scenes of open water and the telltale reflective eyes of gators were interspersed with plants so dense he was sure the lightweight airboat would tip over as it hit the berm of greenery. By the time the pilot shut off the spinning propeller at the back of the boat, Myles's ears were ringing.

Whit was the first one out of the boat and onto the small dock. "You didn't by chance find some of the items I requested?"

The pilot secured the boat to the dock. "Upstairs on the porch. Though how a one-armed man is going to shoot a bow and arrow is beyond me."

"It's not for me. You once told me you could teach anyone to fire off an arrow in five minutes. I'm calling your bluff. Show my friends how to shoot by the time the Prejeans show up, and let us borrow your gear, and I'll pay you for a full bow-fishing excursion."

Myles declined the offered weapon. Though silent, the large bow and quiver of arrows wasn't exactly stealthy to carry around. Once they'd reached their destination, there would be those providing cover and those more directly risking their necks to perform the rescue. Not one for violence, he opted for the latter.

The teenage boy took to the bow immediately. On his fifth shot, he landed a decent-sized bass.

Kendell didn't have as easy of a time with it, but then, it wasn't a guitar. From the way she pulled at the string, he suspected it wasn't tuned to her liking. "Maybe I should have learned to play the violin. At least those use a bow instead of an arrow."

Whit's friend wrapped his powerful arms around Kendell to show her how to handle the weapon. His sinewy forearms made easy work of pulling back the bowstring. "Aim along the arrow, and let her fly. Nothing to it."

Myles imagined the rugged outdoorsman didn't have much trouble landing women. He suspected Kendell had the same thought as she wiggled out from under his educational embrace. "I'll probably be busy helping my friends into the boat anyway."

The light from the cabin didn't extend far into the bayou. Myles tried to stay alert. He failed. It wasn't until he turned to the other side of the dock that he noticed the two tall shadows that hadn't been there when they'd tied off. "I sure as hell hope you're from the Prejean clan."

"Just watching the spectacle. City dwellers firing bows is a hoot." The stockier of the two men lifted a battered rifle. "But if things get dicey, you really want something a little more definitive."

"Good to see you made it, Hoyt," Whit said. "Myles and I will be in your boat. Kendell and Hawk will go with your boy. Did you have any thoughts about getting into that warehouse?"

The man slung the rifle over his shoulders as if it were a baseball bat. "My boy and his friends use that place to go drinking during the off season. We'll get in, no problem. But we'd best get moving. The missus will have my hide if I keep him out too late."

Once everyone was aboard, Hoyt stood on the shallow boat's transom and swung the long oars in graceful arcs that barely broke the water. The long, blunt leading edge of the boat helped it skim over any submerged obstacle. Myles had to really focus to hear the other boat off to their left.

Within minutes, both craft were deep into the cypress grove. Ghostly Spanish moss hung so low Hoyt had to brush it away from his face. Standing might not be the most stable way to operate a boat, but Myles could see it gave the older Prejean a unique perspective on their course. With the engine noise blessedly gone, the sounds of swamp nightlife filled the air. Myles couldn't identify most of the animals and didn't even know if some of them were in the water or the trees.

The fear of crashing in the airboat was replaced with anxiety about the glowing eyes that met his gaze. Every bump of the water against the thin plywood hull had him searching the deck for a possible snake that might have fallen from a tree or a gator that might have swum aboard. As he looked around, he realized he couldn't identify the way back to the airboat. All around were thick tree trunks, downed logs, Spanish moss, and eerily black water. "No wonder the Laroques picked this place.

No one in their right mind would try to get through it without a guide."

"Shh, we're getting close," Whit whispered. The man might have forgone his military training with guns, but his instincts were sharper than Myles would have expected from someone who appeared homeless.

It was still five minutes of complete darkness before Myles made out the soft glow between the shadowy tree trunks. Off to his left, he heard a nightingale singing. Again, it took him a moment to realize it was the refrain of ABBA's "Take a Chance on Me." He doubted they were close enough to the dilapidated structure for anyone to hear the quiet birdsong.

To his surprise, he heard Polly Urethane begin singing "Up On the Roof." She was quickly joined by a male voice for an a cappella duet. She might not be much with an instrument, but she had a lovely singing voice.

Whit lifted the long grappling hook from the deck and pointed it toward the top of the structure. A light puff of smoke indicated someone was up there, taking a break. Myles grimaced at having missed the musical message indicating the location of their adversaries.

Hoyt gave one final hard push with the paddles then sank to the deck, pulling the oars up into the boat after him like a bird landing on a log. They drifted right under the wooden warehouse. It took Hoyt only a couple of quick movements to have his boat tied off. "My boy says there's a key stashed under the fish-cleaning sink. I'll wait down here with my rifle. Anything gets jinky, and I'll hammer on the dock."

The wood planks that served as a ladder squished under Myles's grasp. He was never a fan of ladders. The idea of falling into gator-infested waters didn't help his disposition. The lock took a bit of work to open. Fortunately, Polly and the unidentified man sang with such gusto that Myles doubted anyone would hear his activities.

He jiggled the hatch, hoping that Polly would change her song if he was about to step into danger, but "Up On the Roof" continued unabated. He'd barely pushed against the hinges when the door flew open. Two members of the Mutants at Table Nine, along with Lynn Seed and Scraper, stared down at him from the opening. He gestured to the four to join him in the flatboat.

The quartet of musicians moved down to the boat without making a sound while the three remaining captives did their best to fill out the song. Myles wanted to remain behind to make sure they made it out too, but he needed to stick with the plan.

He'd barely made it into the flatboat before Hoyt pushed off from the dock. Hoyt's son pulled in, taking the place of his father's boat before it had completely left the dock. The Prejeans were like a pair of well-choreographed dancers. Myles watched Kendell scamper up the ladder to let the rest of the captives know the time had come for their escape.

Hoyt wasted no time in getting back among the trees. The song slowly faded away as if the musicians were lulling their audience to sleep. As Hoyt's son pushed off, Myles hoped the music had done exactly as intended.

Unfortunately, as the second boat skimmed over the surface of the dark water, a voice rang down from the roof of the processing facility. "Sing 'Under the Boardwalk.' I love the Drifters."

Scraper hissed in a barely audible voice, "Moron, 'Up On the Roof' was written by Carol King. The Drifters were just the first ones to make it famous."

Myles looked back along the shallow wake left by the skimming flatboat to make sure her voice hadn't carried to the guards. "Do you want to escape, or would you rather provide some musical education to your abductors?"

"I'm just saying it doesn't take a musician to know a Carol King song," Scraper said. "Listening to those guys' stupidity for the last few days has been the hardest part of being held captive."

Myles kept as low in the boat as possible. "Row faster. They're going to be onto us any second."

But the flatboat was built for maneuverability and stealth, not speed. "We'll be deep in the trees in no time."

As Myles feared, that wasn't fast enough. The guard's voice boomed across the swamp. "Get up. I think something's wrong. I'm not hearing anything from down below. Get on the searchlight while I go check it out."

The second boat was still a good twenty feet from being deep enough in the cypress grove to be undetected. A bright beam of light scanned the tributary of the Mississippi before swinging toward the bayou. "I see 'em. Get the boat! The boss is going to kill us if they escape."

Hoyt swung the flatboat into a parallel path between the irregularly shaped tree trunks and roots. "They won't catch us. It'll take them a couple of minutes to get that motor skiff across the berm from the river to the bayou. That's when the fun will really start."

Myles thought having *fun* with an adversary was an unnecessary risk. As Hoyt swung into a large opening between the trees, the searchlight landed full on his boat. His son was just at what appeared to be the main opening to the grove. Two flashes of reflected light shot out from the flatboat in opposite directions toward the trees.

"Not bad shooting. Those bows can be a handful the first few times."

As both boats skimmed toward the far end of the small section of open water, Myles heard the cranking and roar of their pursuers' outboard engine.

"This is where it gets interesting," Hoyt said. "Everyone stay low in the boat. Whit, have that gun ready just in case. If I drop the oars, hand the weapon up to me. I can get a reasonable shot from up here if I need to."

Even paddling a boat loaded down with passengers, Hoyt made the shallow draft hull slide across the water like an Olympian rower. But in the contest with his son, Hoyt was definitely the old man. The second boat flew past Myles like a bird skimming the water. They were securely back in the trees by the time he heard the outboard engine strangle to a stop.

"That'll be the rope your friends strung between the trees. Leaving it dangling just below the water's surface makes it impossible to see in the dark. They'll be some time untangling it from the prop. We're not out of the cypress forest yet, but by the time they're moving again, we'll be as hard to spot as a black panther moving in the trees."

Myles scanned the overhead limbs again, seeking yet another creature that might want to kill them. "I didn't think there were black panthers in North America."

"There are all kinds of creatures in the bayous that few people know about. Now, let me focus on my work. This area isn't to be taken for granted, even by those like me who've lived our whole lives here."

MYLES WAS STILL HUDDLED in the back of the boat, searching for any sign of their pursuers, when the cypress trees and Spanish moss broke into cloud-covered skies. As the boat slowed, he snapped around, fearful Hoyt's arms had finally given out from the extreme exertion, and saw the huge airboat dominating the area next to the flatboat.

"Here's where I hand you off. My boy and I will continue plying the cypress grove just in case your pursuers want to play some more. Even if they do spot you, that outboard engine doesn't stand a chance against the water hyacinths."

Whit was the first on his feet to extend his hand. "Thanks, Hoyt. I owe you."

"Don't be silly. I owe Mary more than I'll be able to pay back in this lifetime. Stop by when you're ready to hear more of my story. We'll pull out some moonshine and have a time of it."

By the time Myles made it onto the airboat, Kendell and her crew were already on board. Before they took off, though, the pilot waited until Hoyt and his son were safely back among the trees. The eight-cylinder engine should have more than announced the escape plan, but Myles suspected Hoyt would use that to his advantage.

Even with the craft loaded down with seven additional passengers, the pilot handled it as though he were on a downhill slalom snow course. His cutting and weaving left vast openings of water between the dense foliage, but anyone hoping to follow the course would be in for a rude awakening as the airboat skimmed above the worst of it.

The newly freed bandmates spread their arms to the rushing wind. At the back of the boat, Myles discovered why. The putrid aroma of rotting fish, combined with what smelled like a hundred pounds of raw hamburger, wasn't confined to the processing facility. After four days of captivity, the intense scents had saturated every piece of their clothing.

Kendell carefully worked her way next to him. "I know this is only a temporary fix to our problem, but damn, it feels good to be the one doing the rescuing."

He'd tried not to focus too much on the next step. "Maybe we should lie low for a while to figure things out."

"I'm not hiding, and neither are the girls."

He had suspected as much. Not that trying to escape notice by the powerful family would last long. They had too many ways of digging their claws into Kendell. Taking the offense might be their only play. At least they hadn't had to rely on her use of the curse—this time.

9

*K*endell had her girls back. All might not be right with the world, but she had the upper hand. She wanted to scream in defiance, to hold a parade in celebration, to do something—anything. As the last of her people disembarked from Whit's skiff onto Riverwalk's green space, which ran along the edge of the French Quarter, each seemed to be full of the same pent-up energy.

"I want to take on the world!" Polly wasn't holding anything back as she hugged each person from the boat.

Only Myles seemed to maintain a sense of reserve. "They'll have their eyes out for us. Tomorrow, Kendell and I will start rounding up our allies. Just don't go accepting any random offers of gigs."

"Shit!" Polly checked the digital display on the ferry terminal. "We've only got two hours before our late-night set at the Scratchy Dog."

Playing her jet-black electric guitar would be the perfect

ending to such an adrenaline-fueled day. "We haven't had time to rehearse this week, but no one's ever complained about the regular set."

Lynn bit her lip as she stood next to Lars. "We've kind of been playing without you. There wasn't much to do in that processing facility. We didn't have our instruments, of course, but we were able to work out some arrangements without them. The seven of us came up with cool punk renditions of some classic rock standards from the '80s and '90s."

Lars put his arm around the spunky keyboard player. "We're not ready. Other than the music, we don't have personas, outfits, or advertising. Going onstage without trying the ideas with our instruments is just crazy."

In spite of not being involved, Kendell liked where the idea might lead. "I've got a trunk full of garments from the 1800s. I'm sure we could patch together something in a hurry. I'm up for it if you guys are. I can't just go to bed after a day like this. Even if it's crap, at least we'll hold on to our slots at the Scratchy Dog. We'll play loud and strong—people love that."

Polly did a hop and skip before taking off in a run. "Then we'd better get moving!"

Kendell grabbed Myles's hand to make sure he didn't get left in the dust. "Come on! You're a part of the action now. Musicians can be kind of crazy when we get an idea."

She was out of breath by the time they reached her apartment, but her determination to play like never before had grown stronger. Cheesecake barked in delight at seeing so many of her old friends—each of whom was more than happy to give her a treat as their price of admittance to her domain.

Fleurentine's old chests weren't just filled with her personal outfits. Suits tailored for a full-grown man in a position of power were intermixed with garments more befitting a gangly boy in his teens. Everyone pawed through the collection, seeking to create personas that would best fit their playing.

For a moment, Kendell thought she should be more respectful of her ancestor's possessions, but she doubted even Miss Fleur would mind the sad garments being repurposed by the bands. "We still need a name."

Scraper, usually the quietest of the band members in daily life but a driving force with her axe on stage, was inspecting a pair of boy's britches. "I was thinking we could combine the two band names. The Mutant Strippers."

People filed in and out of Kendell's bedroom and bathroom in a chaotic frenzy. Clothing was layered and ripped. Makeup for both men and women was applied in thick, dramatic shades of black and blue. In no time, a group style took shape—part steampunk, part retro '80s, and mostly teasingly erotic.

Kendell helped Minerva finish shredding her long ball gown into streamers that extended from her corset to the floor. "Be careful how you move if you don't want to expose more than your legs."

"You just worry about those crotch-less pantaloons," Minerva said. "I think those are supposed to be undergarments. Even with that long waistcoat, you'll need to keep your guitar strategically placed."

"We are seriously out of time." Polly always had one eye on the clock, even when they were on stage.

With eight band members plus Myles running and laughing through the streets of the French Quarter, their group attracted more than a few curious glances from the evening crowd. Polly, always the show promoter, yelled to every group they passed, "Come see the Mutant Strippers at the Scratchy Dog!"

~

As KENDELL UNPACKED HER GUITAR, the antique glasses she'd set aside from the baron's possessions fell out of her waistcoat. Though she knew they might be cursed, the dark energy didn't frighten her anymore. Modifying the items with Madam de Galpion had proven to her that they were for her use whether that was for good or evil. What was there to fear?

As the first song started up, she remembered her promise to Cheesecake not to play under the influence of the curse again. This was different. The dark energy wasn't controlling her—she was in command. But a promise was a promise, especially one made to her dog. Kendell folded the old spectacles and put them back in her vest.

As their first number, Dorian—lead singer for the Mutants at Table Nine—picked "Take Me to the River." Kendell began the usual chord progression. It wasn't a bad choice. He looked a little like David Byrne with his awkward stance and short hair. The Mutants knew their lead singer well enough to keep to the standard without much deviation. Unfortunately, the same wasn't true for Polly and the Strippers. Kendell did what she could to bridge the two styles, but if the first number was any indication, they were in for a long night.

The second number, Wilson Pickett's "In the Midnight Hour," didn't fare much better. Polly was able to wail out the lyrics with her usual bravado, but the Mutants sounded lost. In desperation, Kendell pulled out the glasses and put them on Cody. The saxophonist immediately fell under the trance of the music.

With a couple of quick nods to her bandmates, Kendell signaled for a sax solo. As the other musicians faded out, the long, curving brass instrument took command of the stage and audience.

Polly was never one to reject the spotlight, but even she seemed reluctant to take the microphone after Cody's solo. With each song, the glasses were passed to a different musician and left there until the whole greatly outplayed the sum of its parts. When the spectacles finally made it back to Kendell, she felt as if she were playing the whole band like an orchestra conductor. But instead of standing at the front with her baton, she was hammering on her guitar, daring the rest to keep up.

Though the crowd's enthusiasm was always a driving force in her playing, Kendell typically saw them as one large mass of humanity—except, of course, when Myles was present. She knew he was out there watching. He'd always support her even though he might not approve of her casual use of such a dangerous Malveaux artifact. The realization made her search the crowd for his stabilizing influence.

What she saw, however, made her nearly drop the beat. It was as if she could identify how much Malveaux blood coursed through each member of the audience. Their noses, though not all of the long, straight variety she was used to, still showed how connected each person was to that dreaded lineage. She yanked the glasses off and tossed them into her guitar case.

∽

SHE WOKE to the dim light of day filtering in through her bedroom window. The first surprise was the bare arm around her waist and the head snuggled next to hers. As she realized it was Myles, she settled back into his embrace. Trying not to wake him, she touched his leg to be sure he was still wearing his jeans. To her disappointment, he was.

They hadn't had sex. She would have remembered if they had. But how she'd ended up in her nightshirt, in bed, with him snuggled next to her was all a bit fuzzy. The last thing she remembered clearly was the gig with the combined bands. After a rocky start, the music had flowed out of every member so seamlessly she wondered if they would be able to go back to being two groups.

She had a vague memory of everyone laughing and drinking on the way back to her apartment. Had they still been there when she'd fallen asleep? She couldn't remember. Cheesecake rolled against her leg. If anyone else were in the apartment, the dog wouldn't have been so comfortable.

Kendell pulled Myles's arm tighter around her.

"Hey, you. I wanted to let you sleep as long as you liked." His voice wasn't as groggy from sleep as she'd expected. Some people had the ability to instantly wake up fully alert.

She felt more rested than she thought possible for only a couple of hours sleep. "I need to get up. They'll be expecting me at work."

He rolled her onto his chest with his muscular arms. "Not at seven p.m. You've been asleep for nearly seventeen hours."

Cheesecake jumped from the bed as Kendell sat bolt upright. "What? It's not morning?"

"Take it easy. Lynn stopped by the café and told them you were under the weather. You've been pushing it too hard this last week. That powerhouse performance last night proved to all of us how far gone you were. You needed rest."

She hated being manipulated. "So you've started making decisions for me?"

He sat up and took her hands. "It's not like that. But you have to admit it's been beyond a crazy week. Even Cheesecake's been worried. You know that."

The fluffy black-and-white face that peered over the edge of the bed needed trimming. Kendell could only barely make out the worried brown eyes. She reached down and lifted the heavy dog back up. "You were worried about me, weren't you? I'm sorry. I know I promised I wouldn't use a cursed item in the show again."

It seldom took more than an apology to earn Cheesecake's forgiveness. She stretched out to give Kendell kisses to her face.

Myles, however, wasn't as easily pacified. "Now that everyone's safe, we can back off on your sessions with Madam de Galpion. We should also consider turning over Fleurentine's chest to Luther Noire. He can keep the baron's possessions safely out of the reach of the Laroques."

Though he was probably right, she'd grown attached to the things. "You know, we haven't heard the last of the Laroques. Just because Polly and the others aren't being held hostage doesn't mean we're off the hook."

"Well, you can't keep going at this pace. I won't let you. And that's not some macho trip. I'd expect you to tell me exactly the same thing if I was going off the rails. You're living on caffeine and dark energy. I love you. We need time for both of us to explore this relationship, to go out on dates, to make out, and to just be together as more than paranormal-mystery partners."

He did have a point. It hadn't been that long since they'd shared their first kiss, and she'd been demanding a lot from him. As an answer, she scooched her butt up next to his and wrapped her arms around his neck. "I love you too. I guess I've been a bit of a handful as a girlfriend. You deserve a lot better. Every time I turn around, you're there, supporting me. I want you to know that I'm not taking you for granted. We do need time to just be us." She pulled him tight to her mouth. He was so sweet. He could have taken her anytime he wanted, but the thought of her in peril wasn't a turn-on for him. She reached out her foot and gave Cheesecake a shove off the bed. The pup obligingly moved out of the room. After eleven years, her canine companion had seen enough boyfriends come through Kendell's life to get the not-so-subtle message.

His arms clamped around her like a protective harness of love. Her body followed his as he stretched them out on the bed. She'd had enough boyfriends to learn the moves a man couldn't resist. Lightly, she kissed Myles on the neck while arching her body hard against his. He'd be feeling her bangs tease his face as she caressed his jaw with her cheek. Guys liked seeing her big brown eyes staring up into theirs. The thin nightshirt took only a couple of undulations of her body against his to bunch up to her thighs. She bent her naked leg up along his jeans. Even under the denim, she could feel his rock-hard desire against her inner thigh.

His powerful hands slid down the sides of her body until he found bare flesh. Then he slowly worked them up under her nightshirt until he was cupping her cotton-covered bottom. Whoever had helped dress her for bed had done her the disservice of including panties, and not sexy lace ones. She flexed and rolled her butt in his grasp, desperate for him to start ripping her clothes off like any normal horny man. But he wasn't like every other guy she'd slept with. He didn't let go, but he did pull his face far enough from hers for a conversation. "You must know how badly I want you right now. I've been fantasizing about this moment for months. But don't people usually go on at least one date before they get naked?"

"Stop being so goddamned chivalrous, and get those jeans off."

$\mathcal{M}$yles didn't consider himself a lothario, but he'd had enough girlfriends to know when sex was good and when it wasn't. As he lay panting and sweating next to Kendell, he knew he'd need a new scale. Maybe it was the seventeen hours of sleep, or the overdue nature of their relationship, or the fact that he knew her better than any woman he'd begun a relationship with, but whatever the reason, their sexual culmination had been explosive.

One thing he'd traditionally prided himself on was keeping track of how many times a woman reached orgasm. After the first two, it came down to looking for subtle markers. Often, that wasn't so easy because he liked to wait until a woman had reached her limit before he truly let go. Such objectivity was impossible with Kendell. Her small body had worked his over as expertly as her fingers played a musical number on her guitar. Lightweight, athletic, and agile, she'd had the upper hand from the moment he'd pulled off her clothes. She had danced her hips on top of him like a Persian belly-dancing snake charmer.

But it wasn't the physical acts that lingered in his thoughts. She'd seen inside his soul. Things he liked, things he didn't, and things that surprised him—she knew them all without asking. In a typical relationship, the sex never really got good until they'd been together a few times. The newness was always fun, of course, but learning how the other person ticked usually took experience and practice.

Kendell snuggled close to his side and placed her hand on his leg. "I don't think I've ever felt so satisfied. I could lie here like this with you forever."

He rolled to his side to face her. "I know what you mean. That was crazy. I've never been able to orgasm three times in one session."

"I didn't mean just physically. There's been this growing feeling in me. I can't explain it. Anxiety, pent-up energy, nervousness—none of those terms really work. It's like my emotions have been a rubber band that kept getting wound tighter and tighter. Last night, all those built-up knots finally released their energy. I haven't been at peace like this for a really long time."

Though he was grateful for her calm, a small knot in his stomach made him wonder if some of that energy had been unloaded into him.

~

BETWEEN MAKING LOVE, sleeping, eating, and watching

movies, Myles managed to keep Kendell at home resting for thirty-six hours. But as the early afternoon lit up her apartment, he knew he was going to need other forms of entertainment to distract her from pursuing the damn curse again. New Orleans was filled with options, but each one he considered either held the threat of running into the Laroque family, stumbling onto another item from the baron Malveaux, or leading her back to work.

Their clothes still lay scattered around the bedroom. Being naked with her carried with it an intimacy he'd longed for in other relationships but never quite achieved. The last thing he wanted to do was suggest an activity that would hide her body under her daily bulky attire. "What would you say to a trip to the beach? The Florida panhandle is only a four-hour drive. I could rent a convertible. We could find some cheesy hotel next to the water, spend the day basking in the sun, and fall asleep to the sound of the waves."

She skimmed her hard, cylindrical, brown nipples across his chest as she lay on top of him. "Are you secretly made of money? Some of us have to work to pay rent, buy food—all those pesky little things that make life possible."

"I hate to disappoint you, but so far at least, I haven't detected any energy from some hidden pot of gold. I just don't spend much. I've never felt the need for a grand place to live, cars are just nuisances to maintain, and unless I'm taking a lovely woman whom I'm deeply in love with out to dinner, I don't spend much on food. Working as a bartender, I bring in good tips from the drunk tourists. I don't know. Money just never seems to be a problem."

She squinted at him as if trying to read his soul. "It just finds you like antiques with intense histories?"

"I've never used my psychometric ability for profit. Maybe I should, but we got a little sidetracked with our last experiment."

She rolled off him to lie on her back. Seeing her hands clasped over her head, it was all he could do not to ravish her again, but he doubted his body had the energy for another sexual adventure.

"I guess that's true," she said. "We proved you can read an object's history if the human component is strong enough. Maybe if we spend some time on the water, you could explore its depths mentally like you did when you found that airplane."

He hadn't intended his suggestion to be a working vacation. "Really, I just wanted to get you on the beach in a bikini with an exotic drink, but if you need an excuse to say yes, then I'll happily rent a dive boat for the day."

"I suppose I could skip another day or two of work. We did rake in amazing tips from the dual-group performance. One of the girls would happily look after Cheesecake. They do owe me."

He leaned over and gave her a passionate kiss. *Drained body be damned.*

～

IF HE HAD to drive every day, Myles knew he'd come to resent the time behind the wheel. But as he only rented cars for special getaways, the power of them gave him a special thrill. The five-year-old Mustang wasn't the snazziest on the road, but with Kendell's hair flying in the wind, he nearly wanted to own the car just so he could see her smile on weekend outings. He knew it wasn't the life either of them wanted. She just looked so damn good he nearly pulled off the road to once again physically express his desire.

The miles flew by in the waning light. Cars filled with people making their way home mixed with those who made traveling the road their profession. He didn't envy any of them. As he and Kendell crossed out of Louisiana, the traffic thinned out such that he didn't have to give all of his attention to those around him. They could leave it all behind. If he'd let her talk him into bringing Cheesecake along, he might well have taken the exit to someplace north, far away from New Orleans and the curse that threatened their happiness. He knew she'd object. The stakes were too high. But just for a fleeting moment, he enjoyed the prospect of freedom.

"What do you want to do first after we check in?"

He supposed telling her he wanted to rip her clothes off —again—might not be the best answer. "I'd like to find some little restaurant on the beach. A place that has steamed crab and drinks served in small buckets. I want to get drunk and pass out with you by my side in the sand while we listen to the waves."

She reached over and pulled his hand from the steering wheel into her lap. "Can we fuck first?"

He grabbed her leg underneath her cutoffs. "I didn't want to sound obsessed, but that was my first thought." He enjoyed sex every bit as much as any other red-blooded, horny twentysomething, but never before had it been so all consuming. It wasn't just the physical aspect, though the thought of her body grinding against his gave him a constant erection. Months ago, they'd shared a psychic bond over the cursed pipe tool. Ever since that day, he'd wondered what sex with her would be like. Now he knew —earthshaking.

It was dark by the time they pulled into Pensacola. She slept curled up against the door, her bare leg bent up onto the seat. The salty breeze off the gulf made him turn away from the hotel toward a beach parking lot half covered in sand. She woke from his hand on her leg. "Hey. I thought we'd get a walk along the shore before checking in."

She uncoiled from her sleep. "Perfect."

The snow-white sand made crunching sounds as they walked along the water's edge in the light of the full moon. He was as happy as he'd ever been. "I can't imagine a more perfect couple of days."

"It seems like a dream, or the abduction and rescue was a dream. How can life change so fast?"

He was wondering much the same thing and dreading that their contentment wouldn't last. "We should have brought Cheesecake. Then there'd be no reason to return."

"I intend to enjoy every minute of this vacation, but New Orleans is still my home. You know that. I won't give in to those bastards." Her resolve was clear.

"I suppose we'd get bored with each other if all we did was hang out all the time. Superheroes must find it awfully difficult between missions."

"Fortunately, we don't have to right all wrongs. I'd give up my history if I could. Some days, this obligation to balance what my ancestors created feels like a boat anchor around my neck. The Laroques crave power. They'll never have enough. I don't think they'll stop until they rule the world by any means possible."

It wasn't the first time they'd had the discussion, though the idea that they alone could stand in the way of the powerful family still astounded him. But it wasn't just the threat of world domination that drove her.

"That power can be addicting," he said.

Her bare feet kicked at the sand as she walked. "You're afraid I'm growing to like the dark energy. I guess lying would be a bad way to start off our relationship, even if I could deceive you. Up on stage with that power flowing through me, I feel like I could conquer the world." She reached out to him as if trying to take back the words. "Not literally. But it is a force I ride like a wild stallion."

"It doesn't worry you that it may be playing you as much as you're controlling it?"

She stopped and turned to the starlit night sky above the light-tinged wave crests. "I was worried. I'm not now. Making love with you grounds me. There's a sense of calm I haven't had for a long time. You gave that to me. I won't say I couldn't handle the curse without you, but with your help, I think we can be assured we're using it for our purposes and not succumbing to its hatred."

⌘

THE NEXT DAY, on the small dive boat, Myles would have been happy to just stare at Kendell in her skimpy black swimsuit, but she'd insisted on spending some time in the water. The craft sped through the waves so fast he thought the captain secretly aspired to be a jet boat racer. Reading any potential energy under water was laughable. But the smile on Kendell's face as she braced herself against the railing made it all worthwhile.

When the powerful engines shut down, it took a moment for the ringing in his ears to subside. "You're sure this is safe?"

The captain laid out the SNUBA equipment. "You're a certified diver, so if you want tanks, I can hook you up. This would let Kendell go down twenty feet. That's a hell of a lot better than snorkeling. If you both go with the remote breathing gear, I can keep an eye on you from up here."

She was already fastening the harness around her chest. "Stop trying to protect me."

The SNUBA harness was less bulky than carrying around a tank strapped to his back, but the long hose that led to the small raft that housed the oxygen tanks made for limited movements. In the relatively shallow waters, all he really had to worry about was not tangling the lines.

The sunken tugboat made for a natural reef. Fish of every size and color swam through the broken windows of the wheelhouse. If Myles floated free on the gentle current, he could almost detect the hurried but organized evacuation of the vessel as it took on water more than fifty years earlier, but so many divers had used the location since then that he picked up as many excited children's experiences as those of the original crew. He smiled behind the mask as Kendell pointed out a pod of dolphins that played on the surface.

As was frequently the case while diving, he experienced the irrational desire to swim far out into the beckoning blue water. Somewhere out there, beyond what he could see and feel, was the unknown. With his abilities, he could find what others couldn't. But to do so would involve risking his life in the unpredictable ocean currents.

Time underwater never lasted long enough. The unwelcome tug on the line indicated they'd spent their allotment and they had to head in. Even without hearing her voice, he could tell from Kendell's movements that she wasn't any happier to be finished with the adventure than he was.

She waited until they'd removed their equipment and the boat was headed back toward shore to ask, "Did you find anything interesting down there?"

"Just a lovely sea nymph in a black bikini."

THE STEAMED CRAB legs and boiled shrimp went perfectly with the overly alcoholic margarita. Sitting in the restaurant in his cargo shorts and tropical print shirt, Myles wondered how any college student managed to earn a degree so close to the gulf. Based on the number who waited tables, he suspected more than a few found exactly what they were looking for after high school, and that wasn't higher learning. "I like visiting here, but I'm beginning to see your point. We have work to do."

She seductively sucked the meat out of a crab leg. "It's peaceful here, but not in the way I imagined. It's like what you taught me about reading energy, about how you have to go all quiet on the inside to hear the depths. There aren't any depths here. It all feels superficial."

"And you find that peaceful?"

Liquid from the seafood ran everywhere as she ate. Fortunately, she'd only thrown a wrap around her waist over her bikini. He found her buttered breasts hard to ignore. "At home, history and culture assault me from every street corner. The stimulation is as pervasive as creole seasoning. But I'm so used to it I don't notice it until it's missing." She waved a boiled shrimp at him. "I love the simple way food is prepared down here, but after a day or two, I think I'd find it monotonous."

He could see her metaphor. "For food to be interesting, it has to have some bite. So the curse we're dealing with is important to New Orleans—is that what you're saying?"

"Let's just say I may be one of the only kids who never wanted to live in Disneyland. New Orleans is real. Walt's Creole Square family-friendly interpretation bores me."

For a moment, he considered offering to drive home after dinner, but he longed to have her one last night all to himself. "It's just nice to know we have options should we need the break."

11

For an overweight dog, Cheesecake did a remarkably agile Irish jig when Kendell returned home.

"I was only gone two nights." But it was no use. She was putty in the dog's paws each time Cheesecake showed such enthusiastic love. Kendell got down on the floor to let her canine companion roll around next to her.

It wasn't just the exuberant welcome home that warmed Kendell's heart. Cheesecake had acted suspiciously for days. She always came around, but her actions reminded Kendell of when she'd been sick as a little girl. Dr. Cake, as she called her puppy on those days she stayed home from school, would sniff her from head to toe until she found the area of pain. Cheesecake had the same worried countenance whenever Kendell returned from a paranormal outing, but after their trip to the beach, she was once again the happy, playful dog that brightened Kendell's days.

Myles, however, earned a solid growl as he brought in Kendell's small luggage bag. "Hey, what's with that? I thought we were friends. Do I really have to earn your trust all over again?"

"She's still sore at having to sleep on the ottoman the other night."

At least he had the good sense to get down to the dog's level instead of expecting her to just come around. "I do appreciate the privacy. Some things, a dog shouldn't see. I promise that once we're done with our person time, I won't object to you taking your rightful place on the bed."

Cheesecake continued to eye Myles with suspicion until Kendell handed him a dog treat. "I know I told you she can't be bribed, but a peace offering is different."

She smiled to see his offering gratefully accepted.

Having adequately greeted the real woman of the house, Myles grabbed a couple of beers from the fridge and sat at the small kitchen table. "So if we're going to confront the Laroques, what's our first move?"

He could be so logical at times—not often, but occasionally. She feared he wasn't going to like what she knew she had to do. "They started this by kidnapping my friends. We countered by rescuing them. I'd say we were even, but that only means it's now their move. Clearly, they have a desire for the baron's things. If that's their end goal, I think I need to continue my sessions with Madam de Galpion."

To her surprise, he didn't object. "They asked for seven things. Maybe we can negotiate them down now that they don't have any leverage."

"They still have all the power. I think that's what they really wanted me to know. They had Cheesecake dognapped, and then they upped their game by taking seven of my friends. So far, no one's been hurt, but this escalation has to stop."

He drew lines down the condensation on the bottle. "So you're just going to give them the objects? Even if Madam de Galpion is able to modify the curse, those things are still dangerous. I'm not convinced she really knows what she's doing."

"Neither am I." It wasn't a confession she'd wanted to make, but he deserved to know the truth—even if she was just admitting her secret apprehensions. "It's a risk. If what she's doing works, though, it'll be like handing them a remote-controlled bomb that only I can detonate."

He stared at the bottle as if he didn't want to make eye contact. "Could you use it, though?"

She wondered if his fear was that she was too weak to use it or not strong enough to resist the urge. "I'm stronger than you think."

"I never believed otherwise. But I've seen you on stage under the influence of that magic. Say you are able to convert the objects to only your use. Then we put you in a room with that woman you saw on the paddle wheeler. What happens when you think she has the upper hand? I'm not saying you shouldn't use all the tools you have available, but will the ends truly justify the means?"

He was looking out for her as always. Like Cheesecake, he had her best interest at heart. Hard as it was, she needed to listen to him. "Are you worried that they'll do something to me, or that I'll be lost to the dark power?"

"Both."

~

AFTER THE ADVENTURES of the previous week, work seemed like some kind of alternate reality. She didn't mind serving coffee to friends and strangers, but increasingly, she felt like the Diana Prince side of Wonder Woman. Being the flirtatious barista made it easy to overhear careless conversations. At least seeing her job in that light made it a little easier to get through the typical boring shift.

As she finished cleaning up, the man she'd both feared and hoped for entered the coffee shop. *Best to get on with it.* She poured coffee into two to-go cups. Civility was one thing, but being able to make a hasty escape wasn't a bad contingency plan.

She did her best not to toss the coffee into his lap and forced herself to set the cups on the table. "What do you want this time?"

"Same as last time—seven of the baron's personal possessions."

She left the lid on her cup. "You no longer have anything to bargain."

"We've proven that you're vulnerable. Neither of us wants to see this negotiation escalate. You know about the curse, and you know we're willing to use it. But don't for a minute think it's our only means of causing harm. We can get what we want through other methods."

Cleaning up past family skeletons involved risks. Using the curse might create the fewest questions. If she made it too difficult, unfortunate accidents could easily become unsolved homicides. In New Orleans, such things weren't hard to pass off as gang or drug related. But that might not be so easy if the victim was someone more powerful than a socialite reporter.

"How do I know once I give you what I have that I'll never hear from you again?"

"You don't. I could lie and make promises you might want to believe, but I'd rather have you as an ally."

She took a long, careful drink of her coffee. Nothing the family had done indicated they wanted to work *with* her. "You have a funny way of establishing cooperation."

"We believe in dealing from a position of strength. You stumbled into our world with that pipe tool. Unfortunately, our initial interaction wasn't as productive as I would have liked. My cousins have a bad habit of taking things into their own hands without fully consulting me. I blame their time playing college football. All they see is the play in front of them and not the game as a whole. Had we known of your ancestral connection, I'd have seen to things personally. But that's in the past. We're a powerful family. We're on the rise. And you have something we value." He pulled a business card from his shirt. "This is my private cell. Give some thought to what you could do with our support. No one makes the big time all on their own." He picked up his coffee and left without waiting for her reply.

Not very subtle. She ran her fingers along the edge of the card as she read his name. Lincoln Laroque.

MYLES HAD TO WORK. She felt relief at not having him with her but also guilt that, had he been available, she might have tried to come up with some excuse to have the evening alone. Fabricated stories, even if they carried grains of truth or were for the good of the listener, weren't how she wanted to start out their relationship. It wasn't even that she didn't want him to know that she was visiting Madam de Galpion. They'd talked about her sessions. But his concern for her was like the look in Cheesecake's trusting brown eyes. How was she to dive back into that dark energy with either of them expressing such concern? *I'll apologize later.*

She took her customary seat in the voodoo library of Scratch and Sniff perfumery. The more time she spent in the small room, the more of a connection she felt toward the books that lined the walls. If only she had a year with nothing else to do but study every practitioner's attempts at casting curses. Most were probably failures, but with her lust for truth, she'd be able to separate the useful information from the senseless ramblings.

The lines on the dark woman's face weren't as pronounced as they had been during the sessions. Her eyes seemed sharper, and the dark bags under them were gone.

"Looks like the couple of days off did us both some good," Kendell said.

Madam de Galpion spread the familiar book between them. "Yes, but activities like we're attempting are best done as quickly as possible. Every delay gives the dark magic a chance to regroup. Are you still intent on modifying the curse to these remaining items?"

Kendell knew the question was part formality and part challenge. "I am. But first I'd like to hear what you know about the faction of the Laroque family that wants these things. I had a very odd conversation with Lincoln Laroque this morning."

"They're politicians. If they're offering to be your friends, you can be sure they're stealing from you. I've always thought they have more respect for enemies, though knowing which camp you're in is often a matter of looking at how covert they are with their offers. Enemies make for more circuitous negotiations."

She still wasn't sure of her relation to them. "What about partners?"

"Unless someone's a blood relative, they don't have any. Have they offered you the world?"

She pulled out the baron's tiepin and set it on the book. "Pretty much. I just wanted someone to confirm I was being conned."

Madam de Galpion began filling the room with the scents of wildflowers. "His offer was genuine. Politicians know better than to outright lie without a grain of truth. Just know that while he's giving you candy with one hand, he's stealing your lunch money with the other."

"You make it sound like a deal with the devil."

Her face began the wavering, an indication that the smoke was performing its duty. "And who would know more about that than I?"

As Kendell experienced the dreaded black river, she

wondered what other souls might be in the vicinity. Every book that surrounded her screamed of the torment locked between its pages.

Each trip down the curse carried new currents, whirlpools, and eddies. She needed to know them all, and Madam de Galpion was the only guide who understood the topography. But as the river rapids continued in the deepening canyon, she realized there was no escape from the adventure she'd begun.

Though each trip down involved greater stripping of her soul, on returning to consciousness, Kendell experienced a renewed and growing power. She was physically exhausted, it was true, but she had the inner confidence to combat even the powerful Laroque family.

She waited until Madam de Galpion sat up from the floor before making her way back to her apartment. The dynamic that had begun as Kendell being the weaker of the two was quickly flipping positions.

THE POWER that infected her needed release. Sex with Myles eased the tension but not the desire to command that emanated from the baron's possessions. She wasn't ready to turn over the objects. There were still a few left to be modified. She hoped once she handed them to Lincoln, she might be free of the energy that radiated through her like electricity. In the meantime, those tingly fingers needed satisfaction.

The Mutants at Table Nine were a decent enough band,

and good guys offstage, but they'd never hold a candle to Polly Urethane and the Strippers. The collaborative group effort continued, but Kendell found it more of a hindrance than an inspiration. Not that the other girls agreed, especially Lynn, who made no secret of her growing romance with Lars.

Kendell set up her mobile amplifier at the gates of Jackson Square. She'd never played a public solo performance, but she couldn't sit around until the end of the week, waiting for her band's usual gig at the Scratchy Dog. She didn't give a damn about the tips. She just needed to play where others could hear her.

The screeching guitar sounded like a bad imitation of Jimmy Hendrix. The feedback from the amplifier scattered the crowd back to their business. But Kendell picked out the individual voices from the black box. They sounded like a swarm of banshees. By angling her guitar to the small black box, she gained control of the discordant sounds. Within ten minutes, she had all the screaming notes she needed. She'd also managed the nearly impossible task of clearing the area in front of Jackson Square of people and horse-drawn carriages.

Using the amplifier's feedback as band members, she broke into Fleetwood Mac's "Green Manalishi" with such passion that she could almost see the spirit of Peter Green tossing coins into her case. And like a true blues band, she couldn't let the song end until she'd explored every improvisation that her fingers could pull from the strings. Her vocals carried a darker, more sinister tone than usual. It wasn't the type of playing she'd ever be able to do at home in front of Cheesecake or even Myles. This was raw, gut-wrenching, primal soul music.

As with her experiences in the voodoo shop, she lost track of what was going on around her. She was pure sound. Her body was indistinguishable from her guitar or the amplifier that translated her soul's anguish to the masses.

By the time she had exorcised the musical demon from her soul, the afternoon had transitioned to night. Cheesecake would be expecting dinner. Myles would wonder why she hadn't called. Life expected to welcome her back into its embrace. She listened to the last electronic-feedback banshee sing its final note. The screeching was immediately overwhelmed with applause.

The amphitheater across Decatur had filled with listeners. She found it hard to count how many voyeurs had witnessed her display of raw emotion, but as she looked down, she realized there was no way her guitar could go in its case, which was so filled with money a ukulele wouldn't fit.

Embarrassment had been a hard emotion to overcome as a beginning music student. She'd learned to hide behind the performance. As Olympia Stain, playing with the Strippers, Kendell Summer could safely watch from the mental sidelines. But with the feedback banshees, she hadn't played as her alter ego.

The truth of her performance demanded the equally powerful reaction of embarrassment at her own exhibitionism. She stashed the money in every available pocket until she could scrunch the guitar back into its case. But she hadn't moved fast enough to escape the adoration.

"That was quite the performance, young lady." Lincoln Laroque was most definitely the last person on earth she wanted to see.

"I have my moments."

His smug demeanor made her feel like a real stripper who was still naked after doing her pole gymnastics. "I'd wager that was more than just a musical moment."

"Look, I'm not ready to turn over the baron's items, and I'm still considering your offer. I don't see how we have anything further to discuss."

The leer in his eyes made her think he was about to request a lap dance. "Imagine what that raw energy could do on a real stage—or a recording studio. You know that's something I can make happen. Give it some thought while you collect your dollar bills."

_M_yles had been in enough relationships to know they never went overnight from two individuals living separate lives to a completely open, honest couple spending every minute together. Kendell had her secrets, and so did he. That wasn't about to change anytime soon, and he didn't want it to. Getting to know someone was half the fun of a new relationship. As for the other half, well, the sex continued to be mind-blowing.

He chalked up his anxiety to having spent too much time at her apartment. It wasn't healthy. Time to spend with his friends, or to chill with no expectations, kept him grounded. His loft in the shallow brick structure behind the creole townhouse was smelling a little musty. It got that way if left vacant for too long, as if the ghosts were seeping out of the old clay bricks as moisture. He really was spending too much time with Kendell. Even his thoughts were getting infected with her obsession with the paranormal.

But the problem, of course, wasn't their time together. What had started out as an investigation into what he could accomplish had become a constant rescue effort—and sometimes even an attempt to save her from herself. She wasn't the first high-maintenance woman he'd been with, but the risks she took did put her in the top five. And that was what was really keeping him from sleeping.

He gave up on the sagging mattress and headed to the tiny kitchen for a beer. A little alcohol always helped him think. He loved her and had no intention of leaving, despite their relationship's one-sided focus on her needs. The realization made him feel slightly better about himself. He wasn't the self-absorbed asshole his past girlfriends claimed him to be.

But staying with Kendell meant rallying the troops. Between the Laroque family wanting to manipulate her, Madam de Galpion infecting her, and Kendell's own hell-bent desire to save the world, he was going to need some allies. Unfortunately, most of the people he knew had started off as her associates if not friends.

He picked up the pen from the table and started making notes. The members of Polly Urethane and the Strippers were Kendell's closest friends. They also weren't about to dissuade her from using the cursed items and dark energy. Their band had never been hotter. The Scratchy Dog was quickly becoming the go-to place on Frenchmen Street. The good news was they would always come to her aid when called. They'd proven their reliability when Cheesecake had been abducted.

Kendell's extended family had told her that the homeless

of the city would always be on the watch should she need help, but as with the ever-present gutter punks, their support wasn't always reliable. He included them in his inventory in case he and Kendell needed a discreet escape from the city.

Madam de Galpion was still a mystery, and one that would need to be solved soon. Her power over Kendell grew with every session. She'd proven helpful in answering questions about the curse, but even she admitted her skills were no match for her ancestor. He feared Madam de Galpion's loyalties, and he had too many questions about her. But asking her directly wasn't likely to ease any of his anxieties.

Which brought him to Professor Cornelius Yates. The professor had recommended Madam de Galpion, but more importantly, he was one of the few people on the list who was more interested in what Myles could do than in the curse. Though he hated revising his snap impression of the old man, Myles was forced to accept that he wasn't simply a charlatan who'd conned his students out of money without offering a college-sanctioned course. It was past time for Myles to bring him into the loop, even if most of his advice was more theoretical than practical.

Myles drew a line across the page. He could at least assume the people on the top half to be on their side. But those below the line, whose allegiances were unknown, might prove the most useful.

Luther Noire was likely the most knowledgeable though least helpful person on the list. His unnamed mysterious organization supposedly went back to the dawn of man.

Only the Catholic Church knew more about enchanted objects, but the nuns of Our Lady of Mercy convent weren't any more forthcoming with information than Mr. Noire. Of the two organizations, Mr. Noire's seemed a better pick. At least he'd let Myles in the door of the abandoned World Trade Center. That was considerably better than the nuns only acknowledging him through the gate. But he needed a way back into the man's office. Objects were coming at Kendell fast and furious, and as a protector of such things, Mr. Noire might be interested in hearing of her and Myles's progress. Hopefully, Myles would be able to read in his expression how much danger Kendell was truly getting into.

Lieutenant Joseph Cazenave had provided the introduction to Mr. Noire. In Myles's opinion, that put the two of them in the same category, although whether that was friend or foe was still to be determined. At least the lieutenant didn't report his paranormal findings to Chief of Police Gerald Laroque. Any separation from that family had to be a good thing.

Myles scratched the name Lance Laroque in slashing movements of his pen against the paper. The snot-nosed, arrogant, self-entitled worm had hooked Myles and Kendell up with Our Lady of Mercy convent. Without that lead, they wouldn't have gained possession of the baron's cursed objects. Though having the baron's trunk should have been a good thing, Myles couldn't stop the nagging thought that Lance had manipulated them into taking possession of it. For what end, he couldn't imagine.

Myles put the pen down and looked over the list. He had

some visits to make, and not all of them were going to be pleasant.

~

THE BIGGEST QUESTION, as Myles saw it, was where Madam de Galpion's loyalties lay. If she wasn't truly on their side, Kendell was in real danger. But finding out meant working his back channels. Luther Noire would be the most likely to know of her activities, but he wasn't someone whose office Myles could simply approach.

He ran his fingers along the edge of the envelope as he stood in front of the grand police station on Chartres Street. Somewhere on the top floor would be Chief of Police Laroque's office. Hopefully, Myles was still below his family's radar.

Still, he was hesitant to enter. Myles had done his best to stay on the good side of the law, but stepping into any police station felt like entering a church confessional. He knew he was being foolish. All he was asking for was a meeting, and he didn't even need to go past the front desk. The receptionist would take his letter and see that it was delivered to the lieutenant, and that would be that. Simple enough.

With the plan firmly in mind, he walked past the lineup of police motor scooters and through the main doors. The bustle of activity was as he remembered. He doubted the officers working the always-active French Quarter ever saw much of a break. As casually as he could manage, he approached the attractive woman in the blue uniform and handed her the envelope. He felt like an elementary school student who'd just forged a get-out-of-class note from his mother.

"Wait here. I'll get him for you."

Before he could protest that there was no need, she'd darted down the hallway beyond the metal detector. He felt more than saw all of the cameras recording every visitor. Running out the front door probably wouldn't be the best way to stay inconspicuous.

To his relief, she quickly returned with the man in the overly correct business suit. Even without the uniform, no one would mistake him for anything other than a cop. "It's good to see you again, Mr. Garrison. I'm heading out for a cup of coffee. Care to join me?"

Myles did his best not to look suspicious as he smiled at the camera. Now was as good a time as any for the meeting. "Love to."

As they exited the marble building, the lieutenant handed him back the envelope. "The fewer physical items that connect us, the better. I heard from Luther of your donation to his institution. We're both grateful for the support."

Myles knew there would be more than just cameras around the old building. But unlike last time, Lieutenant Cazenave didn't seem to be hiding his connection to the paranormal, at least not from Myles.

"He was most kind," Myles said, continuing the game of deception. "I was hoping another meeting might be possible."

"There's a lovely little coffee shop in Spanish Plaza that I frequent. It's a bit more of a walk, but if you're not busy, perhaps we could impose on him after a latte."

The busy plaza was as close to a family-friendly locale as the Quarter could manage. At that time of day, the abandoned World Trade Center would be casting its shadow over the main fountain. "Lead the way."

The lieutenant kept the conversation casual until they'd crossed Canal Street. "Most of the Quarter is littered with cameras and listening devices. Once we're in the old building, we can talk more freely. Just answer me—are you or your friend in immediate trouble?"

That wasn't a question Myles had anticipated. To the best of his knowledge, Kendell was at work. But their relationship was still new enough that knowing each other's location every moment of every day wasn't a thing. "I don't think so."

"Good. Then we can get our coffees first."

LIKE THE POLICE STATION, Mr. Noire's office was much as Myles remembered—an out-of-place, elegant room filled with books befitting someone's rich grandfather in an otherwise abandoned thirty-three-story structure from the 1960s. The disconnect between the office and the building made Myles's head spin.

The heavy man in the worn jacket slammed the door closed after them. "I'm not a public library. I thought I made that clear on your last visit. This place survives on secrecy.

Having people just saunter through the front door kind of defeats the purpose."

Never before had Myles been so happy to have a member of the police with him. "Easy, Luther. There wasn't time to make an appointment. I've been getting reports from the streets on some strange goings-on. You know I wouldn't have brought Mr. Garrison if it weren't important."

"Your *job*, Joseph, is to make sure the streets stay quiet. This institution doesn't interfere in daily activities. We're here to take care of the paranormal remains. What happens out there is your problem, not mine."

Myles was beginning to wonder if his questions were going to cause more harm than good. "I won't be long. I just need some answers."

"Everyone *needs* answers. Do I look like an information desk?"

Without meaning to, Myles looked at all the books that lined the walls. If anyone had the information he sought, it would be this man. "It's not like the activities of the descendants of Marie Laveau can be searched on Google."

That managed to shut down the old man's ire. "Delphine de Galpion has been playing with her chemistry set again?"

"Events have gotten a little out of hand with the Laroque family. We've located more of the baron's possessions. Madam de Galpion is modifying them—"

Mr. Noire cut him off. "Shit. Have a seat. This was the Malveaux curse?"

"Yes, sir." Myles experienced both the relief of having Mr. Noire finally take him seriously and the terror that

Madam de Galpion was playing with fire and that Kendell was the most likely to get burned.

The man searched his ledgers for a moment, pulled a thick leather book from the shelf, and pressed a button on his intercom. "Get me item M29848 from the north wing. I checked it in a few weeks ago." He turned back to Myles. "You wouldn't happen to have one of the modified items with you?"

Kendell had entrusted him with the finished objects, though that had been only to keep her from being continually bombarded by the energy. He might be betraying her trust, but it was for her own good. He pulled out the cufflink. "This was the first thing she worked on." *Was it really only less than two weeks ago?*

Mr. Noire opened the ledger and started making some notes similar to what he'd done when they'd turned over the pipe tool.

"I can't let you have that, not yet at least. The Laroque family is threatening Kendell. Unless she turns over seven items to them, well, things won't go well."

"Have you secured all seven items?" Mr. Noire tried to hide his surprise, but he didn't have the greatest poker face. Myles could tell Kendell was in more trouble than she suspected.

He still wasn't completely sure who Mr. Noire served. Myles had come for information on Madam de Galpion, not to give up his resources. "We have them located."

"I won't ask where you found them. Little is known about this curse because so far the objects have been kept out of the public's hands. But my research into Baron

Archibald Baptiste Malveaux revealed some disturbing details—enough so that we may need to become more active in securing his former belongings."

Myles wasn't sure he wanted more bad news. "All I care about is Kendell. Madam de Galpion's sessions are draining her. Each time she comes home, she's filled with this strange power. She says she's controlling it. After a few hours, it dies down, but I'm worried." Typically, those hours were filled with sex, but the two men didn't need to know about his budding relationship with Kendell.

"What is it you want to know?"

He wondered if either Mr. Noire or Lieutenant Cazenave had the answer. "Can we trust Madam de Galpion, or is she secretly working for the Laroque family?"

Mr. Noire took off his green-tinted glasses and set them on his desk. "Delphine de Galpion serves the memory of her ancestor. That allegiance sometimes makes her an ally and sometimes an enemy of the same client."

As Myles feared, it was no answer at all. "What's her connection to the Laroque family? Lance Laroque seemed to have some leverage over her."

"His family has been a client of her ancestors for generations."

A thought finally congealed for Myles. "Was the baron a client of Marie Laveau?"

"Now you're starting to think like I do. Very little in the paranormal world is as straightforward as it first seems."

Mr. Noire's secretary entered, carrying the rough-hewn wooden box Myles remembered as containing the pipe tool. The man waited until she left before carefully opening the small chest and unwrapping the golden cylindrical tool from the cloth bag. Flipping over the blotter on his desk, Mr. Noire revealed a chart similar to the lines and markings on the mat Myles's mother used for cutting fabric. He set the pipe tool on one set of intersecting lines and the cufflink on another. "We each have our own preference for detecting foreign energies. Professor Yates has his contraptions, Delphine de Galpion her fascination with smells, and Joseph and I have our glasses." He put on his green-tinted glasses and focused on the two objects.

"What do you see?"

Lieutenant Cazenave motioned for Myles to stay quiet and whispered, "Those specs let him see the truth."

Myles remembered the lieutenant wearing very similar glasses when they'd first met at the police station.

"There's definitely a change. The pipe tool's energy signature is very directed, like it's taking in power around it and focusing it into an angry beam. The cufflink is more like a shotgun with pellets spread over a wide area, but like a shotgun, it's only deadly at close range. Whoever tries to use it would find herself drained from the exercise. I'd have to say whatever Madam de Galpion is doing is making the objects less dangerous to others but more dangerous to someone seeking to use the power."

"What would be the cumulative effect of Madam de Galpion using Kendell to make that change?" Lieutenant Cazenave asked.

"It would be like exercising. Each time at the gym wears the body out, but once it has recovered, it's stronger than before."

~

LANCE LAROQUE WAS NOT a hard man to find. Unambitious and with enough family money to never need a job, he was a frequent visitor to Bourbon Street's bars and strip clubs. He might even have been someone Myles would have hung out with pre-Kendell. Now, of course, he was the enemy, and not just because of his name. Lance hitting on her at the Mardi Gras gala shouldn't have pissed off Myles, but it had. Even though Myles and Kendell hadn't been dating at the time, Lance should have known that a beautiful woman like her wouldn't be at such an event alone. Myles had no doubt Lance had seen them together and waited until Myles had gone to fetch some drinks before making his move. The whole approach seemed slimy—just like Lance.

Much as he didn't like the guy, Myles was even less impressed by his choice of meeting establishments. Your Father's Strip Club had a sign over the door that read, "Our girls excel at daddy issues." The advertisement made him feel as though a layer of disgust were drizzled over him as he set foot in the club.

He didn't have anything against strippers. Plenty of them stopped by the bar after their shifts, and some he even considered friends, but he'd seldom returned the favor of visiting them at work. He was a service worker, just as they were, and he preferred to be seen as such. Allowing them to perform their acts on him crossed a line from friend to john.

The clientele was older than the frat boys that frequented the clubs on the far end of Bourbon Street, but respectability didn't always accompany age. Entering alone made him feel desperate. As he began to wonder if this was such a good idea, a woman snuck up behind him and wrapped her arms around his waist. "About time you came in for a visit."

He recognized her from the snake tattoo that ran from her elbow to the back of her hand. "I'm just here for a meeting, Josie."

She turned him to face her and gave him a forced pout. "The girls will be so disappointed."

He wanted to tell her to knock it off. He could respect the woman with the five-year-old son at home and a car that was constantly breaking down who stopped by for a rum and coke after work. This made-up persona of a young girl in a woman's body wasn't a turn-on, at least not for him. Looking around the club, he noticed more than one gray-haired gentleman who might have differed with his assessment.

"Can I get a quiet table? I'm waiting for Lance Laroque."

She slipped back to the woman he knew as easily as she would have fastened her bra. "Of course. I'll grab you an Abita Amber for your wait. He's upstairs with one of the girls." She leaned in so she wouldn't be overheard. "He never lasts long."

Myles chuckled more at being a confidante than the joke. "I'm in no hurry to see him." *Probably like every girl in the club.*

The narrow building meant every table was at a bill-tossing distance from the stage, but in the back corner, at least the blaring house speakers were far enough away to allow Myles to hear his own thoughts. In spite of Josie's prediction, he'd finished half of his beer before he spotted Lance stumbling down the red-velvet stairs with the support of an exasperated-looking long-legged blonde.

Josie caught the pair before the woman had a chance to dump Lance at the first available chair. The woman looked over at Myles. He produced a ten-dollar bill and waved it at the harried-looking performer. *Better to have her bring him over here than go fetch him myself.* She favored him with a smile to go along with her nod of understanding.

He pushed the chair out so the woman could help Lance sit. She wasn't very subtle in her unloading of her burden. "Thanks, mister. Josie says you're all right, but if you stop by again, leave this one at home."

He didn't see much point in explaining the situation. It wasn't like he intended on becoming a regular.

Lance looked to be having issues with his equilibrium as he leaned from side to side in the chair, seeking an upright position. Being drunk at eleven at night wasn't unusual on Bourbon Street, but most patrons of the strip club looked to be staying sober enough to remember the next day what had happened to the money missing from their wallets.

Josie brought over a tall glass of water and another beer. Lance reached for the beer. But whatever he'd been drinking earlier, the beer seemed to be diluting the alcohol in his blood as he regained some semblance of coherent speech. "I think that girl really likes me."

Myles felt like he was getting an in-person example of the after-hours joke between strippers sitting at his bar. "I'm certain that she does."

Lance pointed his beer at the blonde, who quickly turned her back rather than make eye contact. "You don't know. Her name's not really Amber. It's Megan. She told me. Not many girls will give you their real name."

Myles knew better. Exotic dancers had layer after layer of secrets they'd reveal to make their customers feel like they were getting to know the real woman. It was all a con. Anyone who entered a strip club and didn't know that was a fool. "I was hoping to talk to you about your family. But I see you're a little too into the nightlife for a reasonable conversation."

"Don't be an asshole. You think I'd tell you anything sober?" He waved his empty beer bottle at Myles before raising it higher to get Josie's attention for another. "Ask your questions."

With Lance in such a marinated state, Myles didn't see much need for subtlety. "Where do you stand with the section of your family that's seeking higher political office?"

"Blue bloods. I hate 'em. Like having money and power in New Orleans isn't enough? Who the fuck would want to live in DC, anyway? Tell me one person who has used power wisely. No one." At least inebriated he didn't sound like he was lying.

"But they have influence over the rest of the family, don't they? You must be a little concerned about crossing them."

"Arrogant asshats. They only look at the opponent ahead, not behind. They defeated the rest of the family a generation ago. Now it's full speed ahead against their political foes."

Myles took a long drink of his beer to calm his agitation.

"The baron's curse is only useful against members of the family. Why would they want the objects if they no longer consider the rest of the family a threat?"

Lance began to look like he was going to pass out. Myles understood. Without a woman's feigned interest, being in a room with nearly naked women in other men's laps was like being the last one picked for a sports team.

"You think too small." Lance pulled out a clump of wadded-up twenties and tossed them on the table. "I'm getting another lap dance. Help yourself to one if you like before you leave. Your questions bore me."

Even with a hundred dollars spread across the table, it took a while before a girl with strawberry-blond hair put her arm across Lance's shoulders. "You looking to have a little fun?"

He stood with considerably more poise than he'd sat. Before he left, he leaned in to Myles. "Nothing is ever what it seems with my family."

13

*M*yles hated arguing with Kendell. He didn't mind the conflict—that was inevitable in any relationship. Fighting with girlfriends had a way of clearing the air and helping the union grow stronger. But there was simply no winning with Kendell. First of all, she was almost always right. That did little for his self-esteem. Then, even when he knew he had the high ground, her arguments were so well thought out he often ended up agreeing with her just based on her logic. But when her safety was at stake, he didn't have an option.

"We've never been sure where Madam de Galpion's allegiance lies. She originally hid her connection to voodoo, pretending she was just analyzing your link to the pipe tool. How hard would it have been to pull out Marie Laveau's journals when we first met her?"

Kendell paced in front of the large windows of her apartment in her loose-fitting nightshirt, which wasn't helping Myles keep his thoughts organized. "Who wouldn't want to keep that kind of history a secret? I'm not saying she's not mysterious. She is. But I can feel my power growing over these cursed objects. Whatever she's doing is working. Isn't that all that matters?"

"Not to me." Looking down at Cheesecake on the ottoman, he knew he wasn't alone. "You're only looking at one paranormal layer. If she can add a component to the curse—your power to control it—why couldn't Madam Laveau have added other aspects to the curse we don't know about?"

"You're being paranoid. Delphine showed me the curse diary. Madam Laveau was very thorough in her write-ups."

Having Kendell refer to Madam de Galpion by her first name only increased Myles's apprehension. "She said there were missing journals, and some part of this curse referred to one of them. That has to make you a little worried."

"You're doing enough worrying for the both of us. I've only got two more objects to get under my control. Then I can confront the Laroques, and this will all be over."

"You can't honestly believe they're just going to leave you alone."

She finally sat down next to Cheesecake. "Why not? They can't use the curse. If they try, they'll find out it doesn't work—at least for them. I know the pipe tool killed Marilyn, but even that event they could discount as having been an accident. The Laroques are too busy securing their power to spend much time chasing down curses. Once they see the silly old stories aren't a threat, they'll move on to their bigger agenda."

He felt his resolve slipping under her argument. "I'm just worried about you. The sessions with Madam de Galpion aren't healthy—and I don't just mean the convulsions. There's an aggression you unleash when we make love after you see her. I've noticed the same determination in your music. The sweet, complex phrases are replaced by raw force. It's like you're exorcising a demon."

She put her hand on his arm. "You keep me grounded. Music is the only other thing in my life that stabilizes me as much as you do. Just two more sessions, and I'll never set foot in Delphine's shop again."

Her words reminded him of a drug addict promising to change. "Even when you're done with her and have turned over the objects to the Laroques, there will still be the change she created in you."

"What do you propose?" Her cross tone hurt, but it also indicated he was getting through at last.

"I want to see, firsthand, what's happening to you. We've taken the spiritual journey before with the pipe tool. I want to do the same with one of the things that's been modified." His proposal was a long shot. Feeling the object getting cursed, and then experiencing the modification, should only confirm what he'd been told by Mr. Noire. His real objective was to connect to Kendell so deeply he'd hopefully be able to tell what was happening inside her soul.

She didn't hesitate in pulling out the latest item she'd worked on. "If that's all you wanted, you should have just asked. I've been dreaming about taking another spiritual trip with you."

He would have been happy to make it only about

Kendell, but what was being done to her was only half of the problem. "Madam de Galpion has said she would like to experience this metaphysical crossing. I barely know how to take you along without losing my sense of identity, but I have to feel her motivation firsthand. With the three of us as one diving into the curse, I should find the answers I'm seeking."

Kendell took a moment to consider the ramifications. Myles wasn't surprised. The sharing of each other's souls had created a unique bond between the two of them, and adding someone else could too easily feel like a sexual threesome.

"I feel like the linchpin that holds you to this family curse I'm forced to carry," she said. "I don't want to drag you down with me."

He understood her fear. Madam de Galpion's sessions had affected Kendell. Even she had to see it. By connecting all three of them, he too might get swept into the dark energy. Once that happened, she'd lose the one human stabilizing force that kept her from getting swept away into the Laroques' power play. "I can't stand on the sidelines and watch you battle the Laroques alone. Even if we weren't exploring this romantic attachment, we'd still be partners."

"I can ask. We'd have to use an object that's already been modified, and I suspect she'll want to do it in her shop."

~

THE FIRST TRIP down to the subconscious reservoir of human existence was always the hardest. Having already taken Kendell into that inner world once, he hoped this time would be less traumatic for both of them. But adding a third was beginning to feel like driving a tour bus down the narrow, congested streets of the Quarter.

Madam de Galpion had strong opinions about the paranormal, but for this to work, she would have to put her trust in him.

"I know you use smell as a way to discover the truth, among other things, but for me to access my level of all-human consciousness, I'll need the room as free from foreign stimulations as possible."

To his relief, she didn't object. "I'm in your hands. In the voodoo community, séances are the closest to what Kendell has described, though those involve pulling someone from that human reservoir rather than sinking into it."

He'd always performed the mental disassociation from his body lying down. Sitting involved a lot of muscles doing their jobs, and that required at the very least subconscious brain activity. "From what little I've seen of séances, you might not be far off, but we'll need to be flat on our backs while still touching each other."

It didn't take much effort to slide the two chairs and small table to the back of the room. Lying down on the wide-planked hardwood floor hurt Myles's back. Even with the pillow under his neck and head, his shoulders felt oddly angled against the floor—as if he would lose circulation in his arms. He was acutely aware of the two heads pressed against his. Kendell's was welcome, but Madam de Galpion's shaved head made him uneasy. With his arms outstretched, he held both women's hands, creating a triangular star pattern, or human snowflake. In the center, between the three noggins, was the cufflink, radiating its energy.

Even in that uncomfortable position, slipping off the edge of reality was as easy as jumping off a cliff into a warm tropical ocean. Harboring expectations while entering the realm of the cufflink's unknown connection to the curse was a sure way to turn revelation into fantasy. Myles's mind was constantly trying to make up explanations for what it encountered. Only by turning off that instinct could he truly understand and connect to Kendell and hopefully get a glimpse into Madam de Galpion's motivations. Some basic rules, however, had been common denominators in his journeys. Each time he'd sunk into an object's energy, there had been some kind of surrounding—a room, an outdoor meadow, a mechanical enclosure—to define the space he occupied. People were often in that space, but their actions were defined by what had already occurred, as though he was watching their history play out in front of him. As a disembodied spirit, his role had been as a silent observer.

To his horror, none of the established rules held up. The soft-pink, playful spirit of Kendell he'd encountered last time was noticeably absent, though he could feel her care and curiosity like a warm breath over his shoulder. Madam de Galpion hovered at the outskirts of his awareness like a teacher watching him take a test. Other than those two presences, he experienced only a heavy fog that blocked out everything around him.

He performed his usual checks to make sure he hadn't fallen asleep. He remembered the young boy lying on his bed who had traditionally been the road marker back to the life he knew. Kendell also wasn't a dream, and her presence couldn't be denied. As he stopped trying to make sense out of what he was seeing, the mass of confusion fell behind like a layer of clouds that was left below as a plane climbed higher. Instead of a bright sunny day, however, he found himself standing in an elegant office.

Kendell squeezed his hand. "What's going on?"

He turned to her in shock. They should have been disembodied spirits who had no sense of identity. Instead, they were bodily present exactly as he remembered in Madam de Galpion's voodoo parlor. "I have no idea. This is the first time I've been physically present."

"Fascinating." He turned at the sound of the voice to see the voodoo priestess in the shadows of the room.

But it wasn't the presence of the three of them that came as the biggest surprise. An elegant older woman sat at the grandiose oak desk with its intricately carved front, with six women crowded behind her, craning their necks to get a look at the strangers. Translucent as ghosts, the seven women shimmered in the soft light. Only one of them appeared older than twenty, with some barely into puberty.

Though the grande dame's face was covered in wrinkles and her hair had thinned and turned completely white, he recognized the pained expression in her eyes. "You're Fleurentine Malveaux, wife of the baron."

Her smile softened the apparent ravages of age. "I'm flattered you recognized me."

Kendell pressed hard to his side. "Why can they see us? I

thought we were just supposed to see the cufflink's connection to the curse. What the hell is happening?"

He was concerned that *hell* might be an all too appropriate word. "What are you women doing here?"

Mrs. Malveaux continued to speak for the group. "We were hoping you would have the answer to that. Are you here to save us?"

Before Myles could respond with his deepening confusion, Madam de Galpion stepped out of the shadows. Most of the women cowered against the wall at seeing her. "I think I know. You're all the concubines of the baron, with of course the exception of Fleurentine, who was his wife. Is that correct?"

Each of them nodded.

Madam de Galpion turned to Myles and Kendell. "Do you remember why Archibald Malveaux took the title of baron? It was because he considered himself the successor to Baron Samedi."

Considering that they were in Myles's trip into the subconscious, he thought the answers should have come a little easier. "So?"

"Baron Samedi, in voodoo lore, is responsible for transporting the dead over the River Styx. My guess is these women were never taken to the land of the dead. This is Guinee, what you might call purgatory."

Kendell said, "I don't understand. Baron Malveaux was supposed to take these women to heaven but didn't?"

"Heaven or hell, we only see it as the land of the dead where human souls are reunited with their ancestors. Guinee is not a place where anyone should stay for long. Doing so keeps the portals to other worlds open."

The women didn't look to be a threat, but Madam de Galpion's description sounded too much like a horror story. "Are you saying they're zombies?"

"Zombies can be called forth from Guinee but not once the body has decayed. These are trapped spirits."

He recognized the irritation in Kendell's voice. He was just grateful it wasn't aimed at him, for a change. "But why?"

Fleurentine stood from the desk. "My husband didn't want to be alone in death, so he holds us prisoner here with him. We serve him still."

The thought of the baron Malveaux being somewhere close was enough the scare Myles out of his psychometric journey. Like being woken up from a nightmare, he sat up on the hard wooden floor, gasping. The two women beside him were perspiring in the small room filled with stale air.

Madam de Galpion didn't waste any time. She was at the table, jotting down her notes in the large open ledger before he felt strong enough to test his legs. Once standing, he helped Kendell up.

"Have you ever been on a trip like that before? It wasn't at all like the one you took me on with the pipe tool."

"I don't know what that was. But I think we're looking at someone with the answers." He raised his voice to interrupt the scratching of the pen against the heavy page. "Mind telling us what that was all about?"

"The dead have to pass through the seven gates of Guinee, and they have seven days to complete the journey. We know where only a few of the gates are located. They correspond to some of the oldest cemeteries in New Orleans. But the seventh gate has remained a complete mystery. Clearly, it's an office of some type."

"That's not what I meant, and you know it. I learned nothing about what you did to the curse, its effect on Kendell, or your motivations." Myles hadn't meant to disclose so much of his agenda, but feeling manipulated had a way of loosening his tongue.

She set the pen down and turned to him. "As payment for my help, I thought it was understood we'd be going where I wished. I do thank you, though, for leading me to so many answers. Your payment has been more than adequate."

ON THE WAY back to her apartment, Kendell knew she was in for another fight with Myles. She couldn't help but feel like a heel. All he'd ever tried to do was help her, but his desire to protect often contradicted her need to save those around her. "I have to free them."

The dread in his voice made her heart ache. "Why do you feel the need to jump at every challenge we come across?"

She held his hand up to her chest. "You didn't see her, did you?"

"Who?"

There wasn't much reason he would have noticed her in the crowd or even known who she was if he had seen her. Even to Kendell, the recognition had more to do with a feeling than visual clues. "She was standing toward the back of the crowd of women like she didn't want to be noticed. I doubt she was even twenty years old. The look in her eyes was that of an innocent child. It was Lilianna Broussard, my ancestor."

He took his hand from hers and wrapped his arm around her waist. "I should have guessed she'd be there. I suppose that does change things. But I don't even know how we got there. Madam de Galpion manipulated my process."

The way his voice faltered told her more than his words. She treasured every story he'd shared with her regarding his youth and how people thought he was making up stories about the objects he held. He'd struggled for so long to find someone who believed in him—the misunderstood boy who felt so all alone that he hid what he knew to be true. She'd found that inner lost child and given him the self-confidence to embrace that special aspect that no one else understood. Taking her on an intensely personal journey into his very soul had been a trust she didn't deserve.

And now Madam de Galpion had taken advantage of him. *Rape* was a term that sent shivers to Kendell's core, but she couldn't come up with any other term that even came close. And worst of all, she'd been a part of it. "Stay with me tonight. We'll figure out what to do in the morning —together."

14

*M*yles sat on the chaise lounge on Kendell's balcony, listening to music from the clubs a block away. He couldn't sleep. The warm night air felt good on his bare chest and legs. Though the action never stopped in the French Quarter, after midnight on a typical Wednesday in spring, the place was as quiet as it was likely to get. It made for a good time to think.

His most obvious irritation was the constant feeling of being manipulated, but quickly following that thought was the relief that it wasn't Kendell's fault. She'd been manipulated as well, though from different sources. The Laroque family still wanted something from her, and he doubted it had anything to do with the cursed items. If they didn't want the baron's old possessions, he had trouble imagining their endgame.

The cufflink shone in the light of the yellow streetlamp

like a Mardi Gras bead that had broken off of its string. Gold or plastic, the tacky glitz was the same.

He knew what he had to do, and he was procrastinating. Since the moment the ghostly woman had mentioned the continued existence of the baron Archibald Malveaux, he realized who was really pulling his strings. All other people, including Kendell, were only supporting actors in the grander play, though having Kendell take point had given him the advantage of being protected by his much more powerful and maneuverable queen. And like a king in chess, he knew he was the most vulnerable of players.

Time might not have any meaning in the *deep waters*, as Madam de Galpion had called the realm of existence he knew so well, but it did to him. The journey of releasing his soul from the existence he knew took a lot of dedication. An intense session, like the one he'd been on with Kendell and the voodoo priestess, could take weeks to fully recover from. Waiting until he was stronger made sense, but in the morning, Kendell would be pushing to modify the curse in the final two items. He could see her arguments. The ghostly women trapped in Guinee could only be freed if she had command over the curse. How their liberation and the curse were connected, he didn't know, but he felt positive Kendell would find a logical explanation that he'd be powerless to counter.

A feeling of dread crept back into his heart. Each time she allowed Madam de Galpion access to her being took her farther into the dark arts. He did what he could to pull her back into the light, but the lurking fear that he too was being brought down couldn't be ignored.

The cufflink between his fingers might not even provide the portal he both hoped for and dreaded. Madam de Galpion had her hand in events that afternoon, and even she hadn't taken them as deep into Guinee as he needed. Perhaps that had been intentional. Going alone put him in more danger. Kendell had been given yet another reason to pursue the curse, but he'd been shown a possible way out— if he chose to take it.

Like a recovering alcoholic who kept staring at a bottle, waiting for his resolve to dissipate, Myles clutched the cufflink and settled back into the comfortable porch chair. He wasn't doing this for himself. Kendell was all that mattered.

～

THE SPIRIT that had been known as Myles Garrison floated at peace on the vast ocean of human souls. There was work to do, but there was also no such thing as time. He found the contradiction humorous. The passage of time only made sense if he inhabited a body that knew its mortality. If there was no death, could time really exist?

Like a pebble in his shoe, the cufflink demanded attention. As always, he could come back later for a more philosophical visit. He rolled over and began the swim toward the shore of human existence.

As with all dreams, the journey from point *A* to point *B* took only a thought. But instead of a tropical beach, he stood at a dusty crossroads. Three dirt paths stretched out to the horizons.

Papa Ghede—he knew the man even though they'd never met—stood at the intersection. The diminutive dark-skinned gentleman with the elegant, tall hat smoked a cigar so vile it made Myles's nose burn. He nodded as if Myles had been expected. "You know he hasn't yet attained the level of Baron Samedi. Close, though. He's been in the ground for nearly a hundred and fifty years. A couple more years, and I might not be able to help you. Fucking bankers, always trying to take what they have with them when they die."

Unlike his normal dives into mankind's collective unconscious, Myles already had the information he needed without having to ask for it. "You're the first."

"Ancient history. I've seen every man and woman who's ever lived. Unfortunately, I no longer have sole responsibility for getting them to the afterlife." He was the first human who'd ever lived and died, the one originally charged with ferrying the dead to the other side—Adam and the grim reaper combined into one.

"Do you know what Archibald Baptiste Malveaux, who believes himself to be the reincarnation of Baron Samedi, has done?"

"I know all that goes on both among the living and the dead." Papa Ghede looked as if the weight of every human soul rested on his shoulders. "What this man has done offends me deeply. It is the sacred trust of every loa to ensure the dead pass to the *deep waters*. For him to keep the seven women's souls for his personal amusement—like they were trophies—is not the action of a loa of the dead. I offer you my help in saving the souls of the women he holds in bondage. Once he is removed from his position in Guinee and the true Baron Samedi has returned, the women will be freed."

Myles suspected he was only getting part of the man's story. Something deeper must have been driving him. "What is your connection to the real Baron Samedi?"

"Some might say we are one and the same, others that we are opposites—my good to his evil. Every cemetery is thought to have its own Baron Samedi. That was Monsieur Malveaux's belief. The first person buried must lie in the ground for one hundred and fifty years before becoming the baron Samedi for that cemetery. You've experienced the *deep waters*. Can anyone truly say they exist as only one person?"

It was a metaphysical discussion Myles would have happily spent a lifetime untangling, but at the corners of his memory was a woman he needed to protect. "How do we proceed?" Off in the distance, figures in long coats and high hats sat atop painted horses, listening in on the conversation.

"Monsieur Malveaux is an imposter who has violated the purpose of Baron Samedi. He remains in Guinee, having refused to cross into the land of the dead. Therefore, his spirit still exists in the form he had in life. But as this is not life, there are limits to what I and the other loas of the dead can do."

Myles feared he'd reached another dead end. This time, the term seemed all too appropriate. "So I must either entice him back to the living or drive him to death?"

Papa Ghede removed his dark glasses to reveal eyes as

black as star sapphires, and as with the semiprecious gemstones, a flash of light hinted at unknown mysteries. "Whatever world you choose, I will do what I can."

Papa Ghede and the other loas of the dead faded from sight. Myles was faced with the crossroads. Returning to Kendell and the life he knew was the most logical answer, but in a land beyond life, such human rationality didn't hold up. He hadn't yet done what he'd come here to do.

Ahead lay the land of the dead—the *deep waters* he knew so well. The peace and sense of all-human oneness beckoned as it always had, but giving in to the temptation would only hurt Kendell. Her love had found a way to hold him to life.

That left the land of Guinee and the one who called himself Baron Malveaux. He had to be hiding somewhere in that office with the women's souls he held captive. Though time had little meaning in this purgatory, back on Kendell's balcony, Myles's body would be experiencing the chills of night and the aches and pains of inactivity. He couldn't let her wake up to find him unresponsive. *Best get on with it.*

As he stared down the long road, the skyline of New Orleans came into focus, but it wasn't the city of modern-day high-rise buildings and congested freeways he remembered. Before him stretched the gloriously adorned mansions and gleaming marble businesses of a time before war had forever changed the South.

The floating tour of the old city ended and deposited him in the same office he'd visited earlier. The ghostly women were missing, but he could still sense their presence.

Sitting at the large oak desk was the man Myles had spent so much time studying. "We meet at last," the man said.

As Myles sat in front of the man who had so much power in both life and death, he realized he had little to bargain with and even less to use as a threat. "You're behind it all: the Laroque family's lust for power, the curse used against your heirs, and even Madam de Galpion's attempt to help Kendell right the wrongs of her ancestors—including you. All I want to know is your endgame."

"You presume to sit in judgment of *me*? Only an officiant would request a combatant to divulge his plan."

He had a point. Myles could hardly expect him to give away the strongest element of his attack—that of surprise. But his response did confirm that all other people were simply game pieces on the board. "I'll stand against you, and I have allies. Together, we will stop whatever evil you have in mind."

His laugh hardened Myles's resolve. "Loas of the dead aren't born every day. Didn't you wonder why Papa Ghede talked with you like an equal? You've been to the *deep waters*. You traverse them as easily as I used to cross the French Quarter from the bank to my pied-à-terre. Even the descendants of Marie Laveau haven't been where you've been. The fact is you're sitting here, not just some disembodied spirit, but *you*, Myles Garrison. Stand against me? You're everything I hope to become. Together, we will do great things."

Myles woke to find he was covered in a cold sweat. The first rays of dawn lit up the spires of Saint Louis Cathedral. His body hurt from being in the same position all night.

Leaving the subconscious realm could at times be like waking up from a dream—the details weren't always as sharp as he'd have liked. This time, however, he remembered every word.

Cheesecake stared at him from the open window as if asking what he intended to do.

"One problem at a time, girl. There's enough going on in this life without trying to tackle the world of the dead too. For now, it might be better if we just tell Kendell I fell asleep out here."

As if satisfied with his response, she sneezed and returned to the apartment.

*S*till half-asleep, Kendell reached for the other side of the bed. Waking up next to Myles was her favorite part of the newly romantic relationship. To her disappointment, he wasn't there. From the smoothness of the sheets, he didn't appear to have been in the bed for some time. Memories of taking the spiritual journey that Madam de Galpion had manipulated came flooding back like a nightmare she was waking into rather than out of. Self-condemnation began raising its ugly head, but before she got too panicky, she smelled the inviting scent of strong coffee. She rolled over to see Myles bringing in a tray, Cheesecake prancing along next to him. "There you two are. I'm not used to waking up all alone."

Cheesecake took a running leap and barely cleared the mattress. It wasn't a maneuver she did in front of strangers as more often than not she ended up humiliated on the floor. Myles was becoming a part of the family.

"I wasn't able to sleep. I didn't want to wake you with my tossing and turning, so I sat out on the balcony, listening to the night music. Guess I fell asleep out there."

She took a sip of the hot coffee. "When I first moved here, I spent many nights in that chaise lounge chair. Since Cheesecake's abduction, I'm afraid I don't get out there at night like I used to."

He sat next to her on the bed. "I had a chance to think over our investigations. I think we should stick to one major adversary at a time. The Laroque family has made it clear what they want, and you've already modified most of the objects. It seems to me we're making progress even if we don't know where we're going."

She could see his point. Finding another cause to pursue did seem like abandoning a fight because they didn't have a good solution. "I'm not sure how Madam de Galpion will take the news that we don't want to return to that netherworld."

"That's the next thing. What I do is very personal. I'm happy to take you along because of our connection, but I'm not some two-bit tour guide." The venom in his voice wasn't unexpected.

"It was wrong of me not to warn you. Even though it was your idea to include her, I knew she'd be trying to use the trip for her own education. I'll never be able to apologize enough, just as I'll never fully be able to thank you for helping me save Cheesecake."

"Keeping you two safe is kind of a full-time occupation. Have you had any thoughts about the Laroque issue?"

She knew they didn't have many advantages against the

powerful family. "I feel like we're trying to stab a ghost with a knife. None of it makes any sense. As cursed items, the baron's things are as dangerous to the people asking for them as any rival member of the family. And with what Lance told you about the ambitious faction of the family already having secured its position, why would they want to further threaten any defeated opposition?"

"But if they don't want the objects so they can use the curse, what do they want?"

She'd been so busy countering the Laroques' moves that she hadn't spent enough time considering the bigger picture. "These things are pieces to a puzzle—that much feels certain—but I have no idea as to the finished picture. Maybe they think they can modify the curse like we're doing. Clearly, we don't fully grasp all the family's dynamics. There may be details we don't understand, like where the money's coming from. Without having an inkling of what they're up to, it's hard to know what I should be doing."

Myles pulled the shoe box of items from his backpack and started inspecting each one as if there were some clue they'd missed. "At least if you have the curse modified, they can't use these things on you and you have a built-in weapon against them. But I'm still worried we're somehow playing right into their hands. Unfortunately, I don't see an option."

"You know, they may not be as evil as we thought. They are politicians." She wasn't yet ready to tell him about the offer from Lincoln Laroque about her musical future. Though it was probably a bribe, the temptation played around in her imagination like a winning lottery ticket that she kept in her pocket, not yet ready to confirm the numbers.

"They kidnapped Cheesecake in order to steal the pipe tool. Then they used it to kill their cousin Marilyn Fontenot because she'd figured out the family power play that's been going on for generations. We *just* rescued your friends from their clutches. And we're only on the periphery of their activities. Lord knows what they have in mind."

She hated admitting he was right. "I guess their actions haven't been the most honorable. So I finish my work with Madam de Galpion then turn over the items to the family. I guess then it'll be their move."

SHE EXPECTED to walk into the normal working routine at the café. Instead, when Kendell entered the homey establishment, Polly nearly knocked her off her feet with her exuberant bear hug. "We got a huge gig. We're playing Jazz Fest! I still can't believe it. They had a last-minute cancellation. We're in!"

The bandleader's enthusiasm was infectious. "Good lord. We've never played a venue that large. I didn't even know you'd applied."

"I filled out the paperwork on a whim. I never thought we'd be chosen. I wanted to tell you first. You're our hard-driving force. We can't do it without you."

A fear began forming in the back of Kendell's mind that the invitation to play might not be entirely due to the band's skills, but there was no way she could let the girls down. *Sneaky.* "Of course I'm in."

Polly squeezed Kendell even harder before finally letting go. "I've gotta find the rest of the girls. This isn't the kind of news to be sent in an email. We need to start rehearsing this afternoon. Jazz Fest is only a week away, and we're playing the first day."

It wasn't like they'd be up against one of the big names. The first Thursday of a festival was normally low-key and attended largely by locals. But playing that day was a major foot in the door to bigger gigs.

"See you at Minerva's garage after work."

For the rest of the day, Kendell fantasized about being on an outdoor stage, playing for people as far as she could see. Famous musicians from all over the country headlined the two-weekend, twelve-stage affair. She might bump into some artist she'd listened to all her life. The excitement was getting the better of her imagination. She couldn't help smiling.

The distraction made her forget her habitual end-of-the-shift customer. "You look happy."

She didn't want to know, but the question wouldn't go away. "Did you do this? Are you responsible for us getting the Jazz Fest gig?"

"Don't get riled up. Your band earned the spot, though I might have helped move the application to the top of the pile. I just wanted you to see that there are advantages to having me as a friend." He had a Southern genteel manner that must have worked wonders at sweeping women off their feet.

She remembered Myles's list of grievances. Even if Lincoln Laroque wasn't the enemy, he wasn't to be trusted. "First you tried to steal an object and ended up taking my dog. Then you kidnapped my friends to force me to help you. And now that threats haven't worked, you're resorting to bribery?"

"This isn't a bribe. Think of it more as an advance on what I'll owe you for the baron's possessions. Having me in your debt isn't a bad thing."

With him offering her whole band a path to fame, she thought a little gratitude might be in order. "You can be quite charming when you're being manipulative. On behalf of my band, I thank you for your help. We won't let you down."

"I've heard you play. I'm not concerned, but bring your A game. There will be a lot of people in the audience who could do a lot of good for all of you. I can make the introductions, but in the end, you have to earn your place in this world."

∾

BETWEEN HEARING POLLY'S NEWS, dealing with Lincoln Laroque as the hidden reason for their sudden success, and practicing until her fingers hurt, it had already been a long day, but Kendell couldn't put off telling Myles about the Jazz Fest gig a moment longer.

The bar was hopping, as it always was on a Friday night. She sat at the end on a bar stool that rested on three out of the four feet. Any drunk using the chair would surely end up falling out the door, into the rush of people on Bourbon Street. Myles was in his element—flirting with women, mixing drinks without bothering to measure the liquids, and tossing bottles back and forth with his fellow bartenders. She loved watching him work, even if the job wasn't the most prestigious or important. Working at the café gave her the same feeling of belonging that she saw in Myles's smile.

As the band on stage struck up "Middle of the Road," he took his break so they could talk outside in the relative quiet. To her relief, he heard her out.

"I know Lincoln is behind it, but I owe it to the girls. Jazz Fest is a big deal."

"I know it is. You can't let an opportunity like that slip by, even if it does come from the hand of the devil."

He would never accept Lincoln as anything other than a member of the hated Laroque family. Myles's concern helped ground her and keep her from being carried away by the offer of fame and fortune. Though she'd never given much thought to the enchantments of money and power— and how a man of breeding could use them to his benefit— Lincoln Laroque had a seductive way of making his arguments. It would be oh so easy to get swept away by his charm. *Good thing I'm not attracted to such attributes.*

"It's just a morning gig—hardly primetime. But you'd think Polly had just gotten us a recording contract."

"What about the curse?" His question shook her. She wasn't trying to keep anything from him, but she'd been careful about explaining her recent on-stage energy surge.

"Polly wants every free minute for band practice, but

lining up all our schedules means I've still got some available time. I want to finish my sessions with Madam de Galpion as soon as possible. I can't tell you I won't use that power on stage. We're going to need every advantage we can get."

He crossed his arms and leaned against the historic brick wall. "I can't say I blame you, but I'll be glad when you're rid of those things. Don't make them a crutch. You play beautifully without the added amplification the curse provides. I'd rather people heard the real you."

She suppressed the urge to give an overly defensive response. "It *is* me, just with more adrenaline. I'm not going to say it isn't fun having that boost, but it's not an addiction. Just as soon as I've got all seven items modified and the concert is over, I'll arrange to hand them off to Lincoln."

He unfolded his arms and pulled her to him. "I'm not judging. I'm just looking out for you. Put everything you've got into that performance. He can't give you anything you didn't earn. Real success isn't a gift. It's an accomplishment."

16

Kendell had spent so much time in the back room of Delphine's perfumery it began to feel like a second apartment, though half the time she was either convulsing or struggling through another dimension, so it wasn't a place she'd miss. The journals that filled the wall-sized bookcases still beckoned with their unread histories. She'd needed the voodoo priestess's help, but as this was their last session, she decided to throw caution to the wind. She still had too many questions. "I keep coming back to why do they want these stupid things?"

"I'm not a mind reader."

She'd had enough of Delphine's evasiveness. "Maybe not, but you have a unique perspective on the curse and the Laroque family. You could hazard a guess."

"Keeping people's secrets is one of the ways I stay in business—and stay safe. If I started spouting off about who was after whom, or what Marie had written about regarding her patrons, or even who paid for my special services, I'd be run out of town."

Kendell suspected that was why there weren't many honest voodoo shops left. "This is different. I'm not trying to hurt anyone—just the opposite. I'm not asking out of curiosity. The more I know, the better I can keep this curse from doing real harm. There are family obligations I carry from both the Malveaux and Broussard sides."

Delphine lit the familiar incense of absinthe and sandalwood. "Nothing ends with one person. The strife extends across many families. By identifying an opponent's weapons and securing them before that adversary has a chance to use them, the Laroques hope to remain safe."

The answer only further annoyed Kendell. It was the same old excuse, which no longer held up in view of what the family had put her through—unless they thought of her as the enemy. "I'm just a guitarist in a local band. How do I get them off my back?"

"Give them what they want. Based on all the spell diaries in this room, that's been my family's answer."

Either the dark woman didn't know or didn't want to know. She had powers but no answers. For a moment, Kendell thought Delphine was just as much a pawn in this game as she and Myles. "Tell me the truth. Once I'm done with these objects, will they leave us alone?"

"Will you leave them alone? You could have just handed over these things weeks ago."

The circular argument of who started it and who would finish it made Kendell dizzy. "I guess, like them, I'm just looking for a little safety from a potential enemy. If you won't tell me about them, what about you? Did you get what you wanted from Myles?"

"The trip to Guinee was very informative. I was able to fill in many of the blanks left from my ancestor. We each play our part. Without someone to archive these journals and answer the long-simmering questions, voodoo will forever be misunderstood. Mr. Garrison has some unique abilities. They are skills best kept secret."

Kendell settled back in the chair to let the smells that filled the room begin their magical transformation of her and the watch fob. *The sooner this is over, the better. Then Myles and I will be free to love each other without this damn interference.*

~

JAZZ FEST ARRIVED in the blink of an eye. The New Orleans fairgrounds smelled of horses, wet hay, and freshly mown grass. The morning sun lit up the few remaining clouds from the night's rainstorm. With the workers scrambling to get everything in order, artisans making the finishing touches to their booths, and bands like Polly Urethane and the Strippers nervously setting up their equipment, excitement filled the air like the ever-present aroma of deep-fried beignets from the booth next to the stage.

Kendell tried to savor the moment, but her bandmates were far too excited to notice much beyond their upcoming Jazz Fest debut. Ever the worrier, Polly sprang down from the stage to walk the cordoned-off VIP area. "The ground's spongy. I guess it's good we're playing early. By tonight, this is going to be a mosh pit."

She wasn't fooling anyone. A crowd covered in mud and screaming along with the songs beat a sedate morning group of coffee-toting hipsters and fellow exhibitors waiting for the raucous evening performances.

"Don't worry, Polly. We'll wake them up." Kendell snuck one of her specially prepared cursed objects under each of the band members' microphone stands.

The bandleader hoisted herself back onto the stage. "You've got our little *caffeine* boosts ready, my adorable little witch?"

"Just don't go knocking over the microphones, and we'll be fine." She couldn't begin to explain the curse or what the objects did for their playing, but every band member had suffered under the Laroques. Whether they knew better than to ask or were too afraid of the answer, no one pushed Kendell about her superstitious rituals prior to a killer performance.

Polly put her arm around her cherished guitar player as they looked out across the grassy field. "We are going to *rock* this place."

It was hard not to share Polly's exuberance. The practice sessions had never sounded tighter. Minerva on drums and Scraper on bass laid down a rhythm that shook the walls in the detached garage of the Bywater shotgun double. Lynn's fingers moved like a grass fire over the keyboards, igniting every musical note. Even Polly belted out the lyrics with a wild abandon that would have made a lesser singer hoarse the next day.

The announcement over the racetrack's PA system let everyone know the gates were open and the festivities were about to start. Polly had instructed each band member to round up as many friends and fans as possible for their big debut. Kendell knew they had all done their best to make sure they weren't the only band playing to an empty field. But with so much open space, they'd be relying heavily on attracting listeners based on their playing more than their reputation.

As she looked out at the faces, she noticed Myles front and center, leaning against the portable metal barricades. Even though she'd just left him a few hours earlier, seeing him standing there gave her a sense of serenity that somehow didn't interfere with the energy she relied on for playing.

Starting with Lynn's keyboard intro into "Something's Got a Hold on Me," the musical set became one continuous number with one song transitioning into the next. By preventing the normal reaction of applause, the band fed the growing energy of the audience. And as those in attendance danced out their appreciation, more joined in.

The magical items worked like emotional amplifiers on the musicians. Unlike previous encounters with the dark energy, however, Kendell maintained her control. The curse was hers to command. But as Polly belted out the lyrics of "Proud Mary," Kendell still found it hard to contain her emotions. She was just glad she only had to pour her feelings into her guitar and not attempt to sing the words about the river and people who were so much like her extended family. Out in the crowd, she saw Myles gently swaying with his hand on his heart. He understood.

She'd anticipated the excitement and how that might affect her playing. Rehearsing had combated that anxiety. Relying on the power of the curse for the performance was like riding a bucking bronco, but gaining control beforehand had given her self-confidence. The one thing she hadn't expected was the raw emotion generated by the audience. Being on stage at the Scratchy Dog limited the energy to those who could squeeze into the nightclub, but out at the fairgrounds, the energy swirled around her like a gathering thunderstorm. And her playing was like the lightning bolts discharging the energy from everyone around her.

The ninety-minute set passed so quickly Kendell felt like they were just warming up, but from the shouts and applause of the audience, she knew the performance had been epic.

17

*M*yles was so crashed out the next morning Kendell was able to shower and dress without disturbing him. With him working nights tending bar, and her schedule constantly changing at the café, it wasn't unusual to leave before he got up or wake to find he'd already left. They changed apartments based on their sexual desire. Hardcore rip-the-clothes-to-shreds scenarios like those of the previous night were for his place. Sweet, loving, mostly cuddling affairs she liked to conduct at her apartment, where Cheesecake could snuggle up once they'd finished their people time.

Kendell kissed him lightly on the forehead before heading out. She needed to stop by her apartment and let Cheesecake know everything was okay. The pup didn't like being left alone all night, but then she didn't like Kendell coming home amped up on curse-infused adrenaline either. And Myles did have a point—it was easier having sex without Cheesecake's whining from the next room.

She zipped the small yellow scooter down the familiar streets of the Quarter, enjoying the cool morning air on her face. There had been no talk of moving in together. She enjoyed her sanctuary as much as Myles valued his. The time for living with him would come, of course, but she was in no hurry. The distance between the two apartments wasn't that much of a challenge.

Cheesecake barked and danced her greeting on seeing Kendell. "It was only overnight, silly. You'd think I'd been gone a week. Let's get you some breakfast. Then I've gotta scoot. Today's the day I'm getting rid of those things you hate so much."

While Cheesecake devoured her meal, Kendell double-checked the shoe box with the baron's possessions, which she'd stashed in her canvas backpack. Modifying the items and using the energy at performances had been an interesting adventure, but she knew the time had come to be free of their influence. Having both Cheesecake and Myles lose that damn look of concern would more than balance out the attraction of being a musical dynamo. Besides, she and the band didn't need the dark energy to play well. Myles was right. It was becoming a crutch.

In spite of knowing that she was giving the Laroque family what they wanted, she breathed a little easier as she swung her scooter toward the high-rise office buildings of the Central Business District across Canal Street. She'd play her hand, and with any luck, the Laroque family would forget she existed.

Lincoln Laroque's office wasn't hard to find. She locked up her motorbike and walked into the grand lobby, feeling like a schoolgirl asking to see the CEO of some major corporation for a class project. After a few receptionists and an elevator ride, she found herself standing in a penthouse office with a commanding view of the city.

"I have what you want." She pulled out the tattered cardboard box from her canvas bag and tossed it onto his glass-and-metal desk.

He leaned back in his ergonomic office chair and motioned toward the seat opposite him. "You look calmer than you did yesterday on stage. That was quite the performance."

She really wasn't in the mood for small talk. "Thanks. For everything. Now that you've got what you demanded, I'll be on my way."

"How's your boyfriend?" He didn't seem to notice the impertinence of his question.

"I don't see what business that is of yours, but he's fine."

"You don't like me very much, and I understand why. But I'm not your enemy. I know you used the power of the curse for your playing. It wasn't hard to miss. In order to have that kind of control over the voodoo relics, you must have found a priestess. As there aren't a lot of practitioners who know what they're doing, I'd guess it was Madam Delphine de Galpion. You should know that her knowledge isn't as complete as she might want you to believe."

Kendell settled back into her chair. "Are you saying you're willing to answer some questions?"

"You've been treating me like I'm the ultimate bad guy.

I'm not. Honestly, I'm just as much caught in the middle as you are, though there's no reason for you to believe me. Politicians are just the public face of power. Those who really pull the strings are seldom seen. I realize I need to earn your trust. Ask me what you want to know, and I'll answer what I can."

"You're using the adage *the enemy of my enemy is my friend*? Even if that were so, why did you demand the seven objects?"

He opened the box and began unwrapping the otherwise everyday items. "I may look like I'm in charge, but when it comes to the elders of my family, I'm still just a messenger boy. Why do you suppose my family wanted these things?"

She remembered how the woman on the paddle wheeler had ordered him around as though he were her son. "Isn't it obvious? Someone from your family, maybe not you personally, killed Marilyn Fontenot with the baron Malveaux's pipe tool. That proved that anyone from your family could be killed and it could be made to look like an accident. Between the power plays, money, and history of where you come from, there are a lot of skeletons you'd like to keep buried."

He toyed with the watch chain by wrapping it around his wrist. An urge grew in her to try and mentally pull it tight to see what would happen. "Interesting premise but wrong. Those in power have much easier ways of keeping our family in line. They expected you to play with the curse. That's been their plan all along. I'll bet right now you could wiggle your nose at me, and this gold chain would slash open my wrist. Isn't that so?"

She sat stunned for a moment. "You expected me to modify the curse?"

"As the descendant of both the Malveaux and Broussard lines, you're one of the few people who could. *That* is what my family discovered with the pipe tool."

It shouldn't have come as a surprise that they'd figured that out. She and Myles hadn't exactly tried to hide their investigation. "But why?"

He pulled a battered leather diary from his vintage briefcase along with a set of copied pages. "That's the big question. There's no secret that I'm angling for political office. As you mentioned, I need to be sure there aren't any family secrets that might come back to haunt me, either figuratively or literally. I'm putting myself in considerable danger by giving you these copies. I know Delphine likes seeing the original source material, but that's too big a risk. I'm only showing you the original diary so you can confirm the copies to be genuine. I could take these pages to her myself, but I couldn't be sure she'd tell me the truth. In return for giving you these, I'm hoping you'll trust me enough to tell me what she says. For your sake, don't take too long."

Kendell inspected the cover page to see the elegant cursive handwriting of Marie Laveau. "This is one of her missing journals?"

"According to family legend, she called it *the key*. It's not written in English or any other language we've been able to identify. All I know is it lists the work she performed for the baron Malveaux. Those in my family who hold the real power have some pretty strange ideas of what's in there. I need you to find the truth before it's too late."

~

IN THE LARGE COURTYARD, Kendell leaned against her scooter, wishing she could scream. Instead of being done with the curse, she'd just been handed another mystery— one she suspected was even direr than what she'd just solved. In the early morning, Madam de Galpion would be fast asleep, but some things couldn't wait.

She gunned the small motor on her bike and headed back to the Quarter from the Central Business District. At least, in the narrow streets and old buildings across Canal Street, she felt at home. Myles would still be sleeping. She couldn't handle explaining to him how she'd been duped into yet another paranormal nightmare. The best she could do was find out from Delphine what was in the pages, assuming the woman could read them.

The voodoo priestess looked about as happy to see her as Kendell had felt in Lincoln Laroque's office. But Delphine's mood changed from tired irritation to excited curiosity once Kendell pulled the pages from her backpack.

"It's in code. We need answers, and we need them fast." She didn't see much point in apologizing for waking her up —again.

"I have some ledgers Marie used for explaining her codes. It may take some time to decipher all of it. If you could leave these with me—"

"There's no time. I was only given the pages to figure out

the Laroques' ultimate endgame. Lincoln implied I might be in danger." His seemingly innocuous question about Myles's welfare had worsened her anxiety. It was as if he was implying Myles might be the one in danger, but that wasn't a possibility she wanted to face.

Delphine headed to the back of her shop. In her brightly colored sleeping wrap, she appeared far less formidable than when Kendell had faced her across a table loaded with burning incense. "Isn't that always the way? These curses lie dormant for generations, but once they're discovered, there's never any time. Acting without all the information creates unknown problems."

"I'm not holding you responsible for anything we did. But now that we have the key, maybe we can get ahead for a change."

Delphine stopped at the door to her voodoo hideaway. "Key?"

"That's what Lincoln said his family called that book. It must have to do with being able to decode her curse, don't you think?"

The dark woman proceeded into her library. "Hopefully, that's the case."

Her words didn't inspire confidence in Kendell. She remembered Myles's recounting of his time with Delphine and how she'd referred to Kendell as the key to the curse. But if the key was really a book, what did that make Kendell?

She fetched diary after diary from the shelves at Delphine's request until the table looked ready to sag under the weight. With each new volume, the woman made more notes in a brand-new ledger. After an hour of research, she set her pen down. "Do you know where Myles is?"

Kendell had expected some explanation of the book, not another question about her boyfriend. "He's probably still sleeping. We had a pretty intense night. I think I wore him out more than usual."

Delphine slowly closed the book. "You're not going to like what I've found. You'd better take a seat."

Since everything had worked as planned in modifying the curse, Kendell couldn't imagine the voodoo expert had found anything that terrifying. "What is it?"

"I called you the key to the curse. That wasn't quite accurate. The objects would be closer to being the key and you the lock. And I'm the one who unlocked the door."

"The door to what?"

Delphine began drawing on a piece of paper. "You remember the seven women we met in Myles's journey to Guinee? There are seven gates to Guinee, each guarded by a loa of the dead. The baron Samedi guards the final gate and is thought to be in charge of all the others."

So far, the explanation sounded like something Kendell could find in a quick online search. "What does that have to do with the curse?"

"It's better if I work this out one step at a time. The baron Malveaux trapped his women in Guinee as tributes to the other loas." She drew a female symbol next to each of the male symbols on her drawing of the gates. "This allowed the gates to be kept open for baron Malveaux, but he was still unable to cross from the afterlife back to this one. That door still had to be opened."

Again Kendell wanted to scream. "I don't understand."

"Every time you took on the energy of the curse from one of the objects, you were taking on a piece of the baron's soul. But you're not the end point, only the door through which the energy has passed. No matter the belief system, sex is one of the strongest forces in existence. It creates life. By having sex with Myles when you were so filled with energy, you were transferring that piece of the baron's soul to your partner. The objects worked like seven little magnets to draw the baron back through the seven gates to this plane of existence."

She had to find a way to regain control. "But we modified the curse in those objects. I'm in charge. I can send him back."

"He has the upper hand and apparently has since the beginning. We'll find an answer, but don't be surprised if Myles isn't at home when you get there. If he is, bring him straight here."

He struggled to his knees in the old slave quarters. His head hurt, and his eyes burned. They were sensations he had missed. It took two attempts to direct his mental orders into physical actions that resulted in him standing. As he looked at his attire, he wondered if the slave quarters weren't just a coincidence. He needed to get some air.

It took very careful movement to make it down the stairs without falling. But once out on the street, his real frustration set in.

"Those are cars," his host said.

"And you're an idiot." The last thing he needed was advice from his host. If he wanted input, he'd ask for it.

The whole scene gave him a sense of despair. Why would anyone think that pebbles embedded in black tar looked better than the cobblestones they covered? Maybe that would be the case if it was one continuous surface, but with the cracks, potholes, and patches, the roadbed looked more like a beggar's garment that had been mended too many times than a street.

But as bad as the roadway was, the *cars* were even worse. Where was the grandeur? They all looked so dismally the same—plain, ordinary, pedestrian. It was as if there were no class system at all. Perhaps that was progress, but he found it depressing. With nothing to admire, why would people strive for better?

He turned down Royal toward the towering marble building he knew so well. Even the high-class street was filled with interlopers who seemed more intent on gawking than admiring the magnificent structures. Though as he inspected what had become of the elegant homes and businesses, he wondered why no one had bothered with their upkeep beyond the street-level shops.

At least the bank had been well maintained. Walking through the intricate wrought-iron gate felt like finally returning home. In spite of his stiff legs, he bounded up the stairs like a kid and pushed open the towering wood doors.

Disappointment was the emotion of the day. In place of the velvet seats, embroidered rugs, and soft gas lighting, the building had a stark interior that reminded him of a prison. The whole place looked as though it had been designed to be easily hosed down. At least they'd kept the marble intact.

He approached the first available teller. "I would like to see the bank president."

"That's a different section of the bank. I just deal with accounts."

He ripped a piece of paper off a stack of forms and jotted

down three twelve-digit numbers. "Fine. Take this to whoever is in charge. I'll wait."

She stared at his handwriting like some arrogant teacher grading him. *Him.* That was a laugh. "I don't know what these numbers are supposed to mean. Do you have a debit card?"

His nosy host wanted to butt in again, but this was his domain. "Darling, take that slip of paper to your boss this instant. If he doesn't recognize the numbers, have him take it to his boss. Continue this exercise until someone gets down here. I'm quickly losing my patience."

"There's no need to be snippy with me. I don't care if you are French. We have a way of doing things in the States."

He nearly laughed his derision. The accent had come so easily he hadn't noticed it. "I'm well aware of how things are done. You have a choice. Call security and have me escorted out, which I promise will be your last action as an employee of this or any other bank, or do as I've requested. I'll wait."

He must have lost his edge. A hard stare had traditionally gotten him what he wanted without the need for an involved conversation. But in the work clothes, he guessed the girl didn't realize his importance. While he waited, he inspected the other clients. Like the cars on the street, they all looked depressingly the same. How was anyone to differentiate those of power and breeding from the common man if everyone dressed the same?

"Lowest fucking common denominator."

"What's that?" The old woman behind him had crossed the invisible line separating those waiting from those being served. The impetuousness of her action made him long for his walking cane. Simply holding the heavy rod tended to keep people in their place.

"Nothing you'd understand."

Her smile reminded him of some old senile nanny. "That's quite all right. I'm not in a hurry."

From the other end of the long, linear room, a heavy door slammed shut. The sound of hard-soled shoes clacking against the marble floor rang out in a staccato rush. The right person— or at least the right person's secretary—had finally deciphered his message.

The woman who approached wore what he thought must be some kind of professional joke. It was as if a tailor had taken a man's suit and turned it into a skirt and ill-fitting jacket. Again, his host tried to offer advice, but some things defied fashion no matter the explanation. "I'm Abigail Laroque, president of the New Orleans Bank and Trust. My apologies for keeping you waiting. This was unexpected."

"I don't doubt it."

She waved the terror-stricken bank teller back to her cage. "You misunderstand. We did expect you, just…"

The woman seemed at a loss for words.

How in the world are you president of my bank? "You didn't expect me in this form. I'm afraid our girl was a little careless in her use of power. No matter. Once I upgrade a little, I'm sure this situation will work out for the best."

"Let me take you in the back where we can talk in private."

The workman's clothes irritated his skin. "Perhaps you

didn't hear me. I wish to upgrade this wardrobe. I feel like a fucking dockworker. There must be some haberdasher within walking distance worth his salt. Though looking around this establishment, I'm hoping for more than I'm seeing."

"Of course. Gottlieb's on Carondelet Street carries some excellent men's suits. I'd be happy to show you the way."

He closed his eyes to fight back his irritation. "I'm quite familiar with the city's streets. I'll need some cash." He consulted his host's memories. "Ten thousand should get me through the afternoon."

She gave him a hesitating nod. "That's quite a lot of money."

"Hundreds should do it. I can't imagine needing a lower denomination. Assuming your tailor at Gottlieb's knows his business, I'll return later this afternoon. That should give you a chance to put your affairs in order. And I'd like to meet with the board of directors."

She jotted something on a piece of paper and handed it to the teller. "We're still a family-run business. There is no board of directors as such."

Her lack of vision astounded him. "I didn't imagine there was. I was referring to the *family*. Surely there must be some kind of guiding force to this madness."

AFTER THE FRUSTRATING encounter with his successor, being back on the street came as a relief. At least out there he had fewer expectations. Though as he watched people scamper along the sidewalks faster than the traffic could crawl along Canal Street, he had to wonder what constituted progress. People either had the gloomy countenance of the working class or the semidrunk uselessness typical of the insane. *Fucking Yankees.*

By the time he got to Gottlieb's, he started wondering if he'd made a terrible mistake so long ago. Was it possible that too much time had passed? He shook the notion out of his head. Self-doubt was a mental cancer he'd long ago defeated.

He breathed a little easier as he looked around the upscale establishment. Some things might change, but expensive, high-class businesses knew how to cater to their clients. A man with hair grayer than his suit bowed slightly. "Madam Laroque told me to expect you. I am at your service. Where would you like to begin?"

He peeled off half the stack of hundred-dollar bills and slapped them on the oak counter. "Right now, I need something to walk around in. I can't continue to be seen as a dockworker. If I like what you have to offer, I'll need five well-tailored suits plus sundries. I'm sure the bank will cover any costs I might incur beyond my needs of today."

"Of course, sir. But if I may say, jeans and a T-shirt are common street apparel. There's no need for you to feel out of place."

He looked the man over from head to toe without saying a word.

"Of course, sir. I understand completely. A gentleman should always look the part."

From the silk undergarments to the quickly tailored suit,

neck ascot, and highly polished leather shoes, the self-image he remembered began taking shape. "Do you have a coat with longer tails? I realize they may not be fashionable, but I find this short coat uncomfortable."

"I'd be happy to tailor you something, but I'm afraid for the day's purposes, this is the best I can manage on such short notice."

It would be unreasonable to expect an out-of-date suit to be available and easily tailored. He resisted the urge to demand the impossible. "See what you can work up. I'll return at the end of the week. In the meantime, I'll need enough clothing to pass comfortably in society. You can toss what I was wearing when I came in on the trash heap."

Before he left, he picked out a comfortable if not particularly well-made top hat. It was the best the establishment could manage.

⁓

THE BANK'S management staff had assembled for his return. At least in the new attire he felt closer to his commanding self. Pity the others didn't share his appreciation for the accoutrements of power. How they maintained control while dressing so much like those looking to them for leadership was a mystery.

Abigail Laroque stepped forward and handed him his cane—the first thing anyone had gotten right all day. He clasped his fist around the silver skull at the top. "I wish to see the third floor. Hopefully, that's still where you keep upper management's offices."

She motioned toward the row of elevators. "It is. I have gathered the people you wanted to meet with in the conference room up there as well."

Though the building was as he remembered, certain arrangements had changed. Cheap-looking white walls had replaced the exotic hardwood paneling and elegantly carved moldings. Any passerby could now stare through frosted glass at offices that were meant to be closed off and foreboding.

He loudly struck his cane on the wood floor as he walked slowly down the central corridor. Halfway to the group of offices, he stopped at the telltale hollow echo. On the wall were the portraits of all the past presidents, including him. "Take these down. Immediately."

"Sir, these are—"

"I'm well aware of who they are. Have someone take them down before I strike them down." His heavy cane longed for action.

With one of her associates, she began removing the large paintings by their gilded frames. The woman had no sense of decorum. Such work should only be handled by those paid to do the job.

He ran his hand over the smooth, bare wall. The change would have been undetectable to anyone not aware of the modification. But even under layers of paint, he could feel the difference in texture. Those around him scattered as he stepped back and swung his cane with all the force of a wrecking ball. The relatively thin layer of plaster crumbled to the ground as if it had been made of eggshells.

There, hidden for centuries, was the ornately carved

doorframe of his office. The large mahogany doors still displayed the elegant *M*s with skulls at the corners as though they'd just been engraved. Inscribed above the doors in the heavy wooden frame were the words, "The Seventh Gate of Guinee."

"Time to get to work."

endell had never felt so lost and alone in her life. Myles hadn't been at his apartment, just as Delphine had guessed. In desperation, Kendell returned to her apartment to hold Cheesecake tight in her arms. "Why do I lose everyone I care about? First you, then the band, and now Myles." Tears flowed down her cheeks to be absorbed by the pup's shaggy coat.

Cheesecake arched her back and kissed away Kendell's tears.

"I should have listened to you. Each time I worked on one of those objects, you'd growl at me when I got home. If I performed a killer gig under the power of the curse, you gave me your judgmental stare. That's probably why I preferred having sex with Myles at his place. It wasn't the sex that bothered you—it was what I was doing to him."

No one had a better understanding of the curse's power than Cheesecake. She'd had the pipe tool inside her. Kendell remembered the wolflike growling she'd set loose on her abductors. Again, Kendell condemned herself for not listening to her life companion. "I'm going to get him back. I rescued you, and I helped free my friends. Those things took physical courage, and you know that's not my strong point. Saving Myles will be different. I can do this paranormal adventure. You'll see."

She'd need help, and she knew just the seven women who might join her. To find them, however, would mean taking a voyage into the realm she'd only visited with Myles's guidance. Assuming Kendell could make the journey, at least one of the ghostly apparitions would need convincing.

Fleurentine Malveaux's trunks still filled half of Kendell's living room. What was left of the baron's possessions were either meaningless items or clothing, but it wasn't his stuff she was after. To contact Miss Fleur, as the nuns had called her, would involve finding her without the influence of the curse.

At the bottom of the chest of frilly antique dresses was a small leather case filled with expensive jewelry. Kendell inspected the diamond-encrusted broaches and blue sapphire necklaces. These were not the possessions of a woman who would sequester herself in a convent. Kendell remembered the pictures from the family albums. Fleurentine's early years married to Archibald Malveaux had been similar to those of a gutter waif plucked from poverty and transformed into the belle of New Orleans society. These baubles would have come from her husband during a happier time of her life, but they wouldn't be representative of the woman Kendell hoped to reach. She tossed the box with expensive jewelry onto her nightstand.

Lance Laroque had taken every diary he could find before Kendell had gained access to Miss Fleur's possessions, but at the bottom of the half-empty trunk that held random correspondences, she found a small case of pastel sticks. Unpretentious brown folders were scattered across the bottom of the trunk. She opened the first and found drawings of a young girl. The emotion poured into the flat sheet of vellum was unmistakable. Blond, blue eyed, and with an expression of joy, the child had to be Serephine Malveaux, the daughter who had been the first to fall under the curse.

Kendell reverently removed the drawings from the file and spread them out on the coffee table. Serephine had been the entry point for the exploration that had resulted in Kendell being bound to the curse. Maybe she could also be the way out. A page was filled with studies of the girl's sky-blue eyes and nothing else—just the expression of innocent joy that sparkled in them. Kendell pulled it from the rest and returned to her bedroom.

Cheesecake hadn't moved from her command post on the end of the bed. Kendell remembered the first thing Myles had taught her about exploring the inner journey: she needed a core memory to help guide her back to her life. For that, she used the treasured image of the first time she and her pup had met eleven years earlier.

She ruffled the shaggy black-and-white head. "I don't mind you staying there. Just don't freak out when I get really quiet." She would have liked to promise the dog that she knew what she was doing, but lying to Cheesecake wasn't part of their relationship.

She eased back down on the bed and sought the most muscle-relaxing position she could find. As if doing likewise, Cheesecake stretched out against her leg. Kendell clutched the drawing to her chest and began the mantra Myles had taught her. *I am what I am.*

At first, the words didn't make much sense for separating her soul from her body. What was she? A lead guitarist for an up-and-coming band, a server of coffee, the much-loved caregiver to one of God's greatest creations—a dog—and the lover of a seriously misunderstood guy. As the descriptions circled around her thoughts, she realized they were only the outward manifestations of what she wanted out of life. Like the person operating the movie camera, she had to find that shy hidden soul who was really behind the scenes.

That realization was like falling into a bottomless pothole in one of New Orleans's streets. Everything that she'd used to define her life was only what she presented to the world.

The drawing worked like a magnet to another life just as the pipe tool had done with Myles. She stood in the doorway of a large parlor filled with children's toys from a long time ago. As the little girl on the floor interacted with her dolls, her mother raised a cloud of blue dust from her feverish scraping of pastel stick to paper. The scene warmed Kendell's heart.

It wasn't supposed to. As a disembodied spirit, she was there to observe. Experiencing her own emotions would separate her from the scene. That was what Myles had said. The memory of him should have taken her even further from her objective, yet she remained in the doorway of the long-gone mansion.

She wasn't alone. An animal half her size stood at attention next to her. She reached over and petted the short, straight hair of the black-and-white wolf. "You're not supposed to be here."

To her relief, the animal didn't respond with words but snuggled her head against Kendell's hip. The love and protection she felt from Cheesecake was even more prominent in this world of pure essence.

Though Cheesecake didn't answer, another woman's voice startled Kendell into spinning around to see who had snuck up behind her. "I knew you'd show up eventually. I appreciate that you chose this memory. My love of that child is still an open wound even after all this time."

"I didn't mean to cause you pain, but of all your possessions, I felt the most emotion from your drawings."

The woman's eyes glistened, but from her smile, Kendell knew they weren't tears of sorrow. "From the moment I saw you in my husband's office, I knew you'd need my help. That boy of yours is quite talented in crossing into Guinee, but I figured you might need a little assistance meeting me without him. Those pictures I drew so long ago may be the only bridge between us that has a chance of working." The old woman in drab convent attire turned to Cheesecake. "But did you really think it necessary to bring your spirit wolf?"

Though Cheesecake was a wolf with a commanding

presence, one that would create fear in most people, Miss Fleur scratched her ear. The old dog bent her head into the hand and exhibited all her usual responses of joy at the woman's attention.

"She came of her own free will. I think she was just curious."

Miss Fleur patted the black-and-white head. "She's not a bad companion. I wish I'd had such a loyal friend in life. The day may come where you'll be glad to have her by your side, either in this realm or that of the living. But I doubt you came here for me to tell you what you already know."

"The baron has taken possession of Myles." Though she knew it to be true, expressing the thought gave Kendell a profound sense of dread. This had been her fault, and that guilt hung like a shadow around her.

With ghostly pale-gray eyes, Fleurentine inspected Kendell for so long that she felt naked under the woman's stare. "You could command me, but you're not doing that."

"I need your help—you and the others. I have control of the curse, but using it would make me no better than the force I hope to defeat."

Fleurentine nodded as if she'd figured out Kendell's objective. "But I'm not the person you came to see."

"I'm hoping you can help me convince her."

"I'll take you to her, but you might want to leave your pup back among the living."

Kendell turned to her wolf. "I'm okay, girl. You proved your point. I'm never alone, not even in this spiritual realm. But if you appear like the imposing creature I know you to be, you're going to scare some people. Run along back to the bed. I'll be back soon."

Cheesecake whined at not being allowed to stay, but she reluctantly turned toward the hallway and vanished back to the land of the living.

The heartwarming scene of mother and daughter dissolved and was replaced by the office Kendell had visited with Myles and Delphine. There was a change Kendell found hard to identify. The walls appeared more substantial, though previously she hadn't thought them to be illusions. *I'm imagining things.* The thought made her feel even closer to Myles. So many people had discounted his reality as daydreaming.

The girl who stood behind the desk looked like a teenager. "You've got no right to ask me." As she cowered in the corner, Kendell felt real pity for the frightened youth.

"Lilianna Broussard, you know I wouldn't if there was another choice."

"You've got no *right*. I don't care if you are my great-great-granddaughter. You have no idea what he's done to me. After he used me in life, he sold me in death to Baron Kriminel. For a hundred and fifty years, I've been a slave. Now that the baron finally has what he wants, I can be free. I won't go back."

For a moment, Kendell thought she understood what her own parents had gone through raising her. The obstinate young woman knew she was right and wouldn't let anyone tell her differently. It was a reaction Kendell was very familiar with from her childhood.

"I'm not asking you to go back to being bound to one of

the loas of the dead. If we can send Archibald to the afterlife, you all can be free to finally cross over."

"Right. But first you want him back here in Guinee, back where he has power over us. Fleur, you know how it is. You can't agree to having *him* back with us."

Having lived a full life, Fleurentine made her case with far fewer dramatics. "Turning him loose in the land of the living is not an answer to our situation. Right now, he's free to enslave even more young women. If we don't do all we can to stop him, we will be to blame. In life, I watched as he stole you and the others from your families, raped you, manipulated your emotions, let you keep your children, but never let you forget who their father was, and now he holds you in this purgatory. I won't make the mistake of sitting idly by again."

Lilianna crossed her arms in a huff. "That's your burden, not mine."

"I can do this, Lilianna, but only with your help," Kendell said. "I can end the Malveaux curse."

"End it? Who do you think holds the curse in their hands? It's us—the sisterhood of girls who gave Marie Laveau the power to create the spell and stand watch over it to this day. It's all we have to keep him in check."

Kendell wished she could hold the frightened girl in her arms, but under that fear, she saw the same raw determination that she knew within herself. "I know the burden you think you carry—the promise you made so long ago—and I can assure you that you did save your brother. I've met his descendants. They call you *the angel*. Your sacrifice enabled him to live a full life, even if it cut yours short. I invite you to read my mind so you'll see. Those people love and revere you."

Even with Myles taking her into the realm of human consciousness, she'd never before experienced having someone else infect her thoughts. As Lilianna moved into her mind, Kendell understood that the scared, angry girl carried a maternal protectiveness that came from watching after her younger brother. Seeing her beloved sibling's line stretch from the young boy to the clan on the other side of the river filled Kendell's heart with warmth, but it wasn't her emotion—it was Lilianna's. *They'll be in danger. All of them. The baron Malveaux won't rest until he's hunted them down just to spite* you. *He'll do the same to all of those you call sisters.*

Lilianna separated herself from Kendell. "Don't presume to manipulate me. Just because I've watched over those before you doesn't mean I'm a pushover. I've done what I can."

Never before had Kendell considered her need to protect those around her as a maternal instinct, but with Lilianna standing before her, she recognized the root of what Myles had called her *superhero spirit.* "All I'm asking is for your help so I can continue the work you started so long ago."

20

_M_yles imagined this was what it must be like to be a goldfish in a bowl, staring at people who were free to do as they pleased. Other than observing or ignoring what the baron was doing with his body, he had no free will.

As if being trapped weren't bad enough, he had to endure the endless talking of the rich and powerful. _"Why can't you go out on a yacht or secret nightclub that caters only to the rich? Why does it have to be another boring meeting?"_

"Shut up, and maybe you'll learn something. Or remain ignorant if you prefer. Either way, keep quiet."

Everyone in the office suite deferred to the elegant, mature woman at the head of the table. "We're pleased to have you back among us. Our most pressing challenge is funneling money to our congressional campaign. It's not enough for Lincoln simply to win the seat. He must be seen on the national stage. That type of advertisement takes money."

"Stop." The word echoed around Myles's head with even more command than the deep baritone that filled the room. "You're chasing after politics?"

"Precisely. Once you help us—"

"I am not here to help you. I am the baron Malveaux. Since when does money pursue political power? Mayors and senators came on bended knee to ask my favors to secure their temporary illusions of command. You would throw away all that I've built for a moment of glory?"

In spite of starting off on the defensive, the woman knew how to command a room. "I think you'll find times have changed. Washington and New York are the centers of power. We need to establish a presence—"

"Don't treat me like a fool. This mind I'm in contains enough information on current affairs, even if he did focus more on the party aspect than important business concerns. What I want to know is why the family's power base is *still* limited to New Orleans. Politics? Exposure? When did the Laroque family begin thinking so small? The time for safe, gradual forays into the upper regions of the establishment are long past. No one ever made it to the top by playing by the rules." He looked around at the subordinates in disgust. "Except perhaps those in my own family."

Myles could see the anger growing in the woman's eyes even if the baron who was running his body didn't notice or care. "We summoned you—"

"*You* summoned *me?*" The baron's ice-cold laugh was pitched to shut down discussion. "For a hundred and fifty years, I've watched this family squander every opportunity for greatness. I suppose the old adage is correct: if you want something done right, you have to do it yourself. I am not here to help *you*. You are here to serve me. Never forget that I am a loa of the dead."

The woman sagged into her chair like a student who'd just had her dissertation torn to shreds by a sadistic professor. "What do you have in mind?"

"The South is about to rise again, only this time we'll fight on our own terms. We'll take what others consider weaknesses and make them our strengths. As far as the Union is concerned, we're still a beaten, simple, uneducated people. Rather than combat that image, we'll embrace it—to their horror. Their underestimation of us will be their undoing. By the time they realize what's happening, they'll be powerless to stop us. Senator? No. We're running Lincoln Laroque as president, but he'll just be the distraction we use while we gather the economic forces. For a bank, you people have a woeful misunderstanding of where the real power lies."

Like a prisoner in a dungeon pulling at the bars of his cell in frustration, Myles railed at the evil he saw brewing in the baron's thoughts.

KENDELL MUST KNOW *what's happened.* The thought was the only hope Myles could cling to. Something must have gone wrong with the curse, but he couldn't figure out what. The baron wasn't making any attempt at maintaining Myles's normal life. That had to work in Myles's favor. Kendell wouldn't have to work too hard convincing Madam de Galpion or Luther Noire or Lieutenant Cazenave that something was wrong. Still, he wondered if any of them would have any clue as to what to do about the possession.

Nothing about modern-day New Orleans seemed to be to the baron's tastes. Even if they hadn't been sharing a mind and body, Myles would have figured that out pretty quickly. As they walked down the middle of Royal Street, the baron attempted to put as much distance as he could between himself and the common man. He turned his nose up at the expensive restaurants filled with noisy families on vacation. "How does a society function like this?"

The baron might have been talking to himself, but Myles figured there was no harm in answering. *"It's called social equality. Take the idea of all people being equal and run it to its logical conclusion."*

"It's all men *are considered equal. If you intend to instruct me, at least get the terms right."* The smug voice in Myles's head, freed from the restrictions of vocal cords, oozed aristocratic contempt.

"Yeah, well, we no longer rape the wives and daughters of our enemies, in case you hadn't noticed."

He couldn't detect even a hint of sarcasm in the response. *"That's a shame. From what I can see, complete equality is a bore. I appreciate the challenge of having a woman be in charge in the boardroom but only so I can enjoy taking her down to the depths of my depravity. A man, even you, has a fundamental biological need to dominate. Women aren't born* with that drive. They may learn it, but they will never be consumed by it as we are."

"Men and women can do more together than as adversaries. Women have a unique view of life. Respecting all races, genders, and religions makes our society stronger. We're the envy of—"

"Oh, do shut up. I have no interest in being envied. If I've learned anything after all those years in the ground, it's that people hold on to concepts too much without considering the basis of those ideas. There's nothing noble about having other people look up to you if it's all a façade."

Myles feared the baron wasn't totally wrong—complete equality tended to be more of a longed-for illusion than an achievable reality—but he had to believe having a higher goal helped humanity evolve. "Face it, there's no room for your antiquated thinking in this reality."

"You still don't get it, do you? The rich control the powerful, who sell the vision to the masses. There is no equality in any meaningful sense. Money creates what you call reality. Freedom, equality, social justice—they're all just carrots to keep the hamsters on the wheel."

As if it weren't bad enough that Myles was trapped in his own body, now he had to endure a lecture on the sins of morality. He began humming to himself so he wouldn't have to listen.

"Knock that off. It's irritating."

Myles smiled at having found a way to strike back. "Sucks when the downtrodden start rising up, doesn't it?"

∾

MYLES STILL HAD one advantage over the baron. Being in the same body meant he had access to the *deep waters*. And as the baron insisted on being in charge in life, that left Myles free to explore the ocean of consciousness.

Papa Ghede stood at the familiar crossroads. "I hope having the baron take possession of your body wasn't what you had intended."

Myles couldn't find humor in the sarcasm. "*I* didn't do anything. How do I get out of this mess?"

"Monsieur Malveaux is a cunning adversary—in life as well as death. It'll take a combination of the living and the dead to defeat him."

As an unwilling vessel for the baron, Myles was trapped between the two realms, with little to offer either. "What can I do?" he asked in despair.

"When the time comes, ride with me to the seven gates. Archibald Malveaux isn't yet a loa, so for him to escape the land of the dead and return to the living is an embarrassment to us all."

Myles had trouble figuring out where he belonged in the two worlds. "But I'm still alive, aren't I? What will happen to me if I pass through all the gates?"

"You still have a living body, which I assume you wish to keep. You'll need to present offerings to each of the loas of the dead to prevent them from claiming your soul. Since you don't have control of your body, you'll need someone to put the items on the various tombs for you at the correct time."

"I know someone who can help if I can reach her." He'd escorted Kendell to the secret realm, but taking the journey on her own would be very different from doing it with him as her guide.

Papa Ghede drew a picture of a cross in the dust. "Remember this symbol. It's the veve of Baron Samedi. With it, your friend can identify the seven gates."

Myles stared at the crosses and lines. "How is she supposed to make anything out of that? I'm here in Guinee, and it makes no sense to me."

"It's all I have that's translatable into the world of the living. There is another being, though, who can help your friend on her quest—the true Baron Samedi's wife, Maman Brigitte. Find your friend, and tell her to seek out Brigitte. The veve that marks her will help your friend decipher the baron's symbol."

Myles bowed to the short man, his only hope of returning to a normal life. "Thank you."

Papa Ghede's mysterious smile left him wondering what wasn't being said.

As a being of pure energy floating around Kendell's bedroom while she attempted to fall asleep, Myles suspected he might understand how ghosts felt. He didn't want to freak her out, but he needed to talk to her. She'd only be in the half-asleep, spiritually free state for a matter of seconds.

"Hey, don't wake up, but I need to talk to you."

Her inner thoughts of the day at work—and her worry about him—were morphing into having a picnic on a sunny day with him and Cheesecake. He was losing her to sleep.

Cheesecake, however, sat up on the bed to stare directly at him as he hovered over the bed. She didn't growl, but her fearful whine managed to bring Kendell out of her sleep. "What is it, girl? Did you have a bad dream?"

The pup gave Kendell a kiss on the cheek and turned back toward Myles. Kendell looked up, but he knew she only saw the wood-beamed ceiling.

"How am I supposed to reach you?"

Cheesecake gave a single bark reply, but he doubted Kendell would understand.

At least the dog might hear him. *"She needs to almost fall asleep. Do you think you could cuddle next to her? If she drifts off, nuzzle her back to that half-asleep state."*

Cheesecake got up and circled a spot next to Kendell then plopped down so firmly it looked like she was forcing Kendell off the bed.

"Okay, girl. I get it. I missed you too." She petted the shaggy head, but the dog's dark-brown eyes were still turned to Myles, and he knew the pup would do what she could to unite her two people.

He felt helpless to reach Kendell. She would need to find him, but where should he wait? As Cheesecake closed her sleepy eyes, he feared he was about to lose his one potential assistant. Instead of drifting off into dreams of chasing squirrels, a much younger, fitter dog smiled in front of him and barked in his spirit realm. The pup turned and started running off but turned to make sure he knew he should follow.

"I'm coming, sweet girl."

In the middle of the grassy field was a red-and-black-checkered blanket crowded with plates of hamburgers, potato salad, and dog treats. Cheesecake raced for the spread like a pup on a mission.

He sat on the edge of the blanket, waiting. Instead of him being the ghost, it was Kendell who appeared out of thin air.

"About time," he said. "The burgers were getting cold."

Tears formed in her eyes. "I miss you so much. Why can't this be real?"

He got up and took her in his arms. "Don't wake up, but this is real. Remember everything I taught you about traveling in that other dimension? Well, that's where I am. Cheesecake made sure I got into this dream before you arrived. I think she knew you'd follow her. I need your help."

Kendell hugged him hard, pressing her whole body against his. "It's really you? I'm not just imagining this?"

"Are you awake or asleep?"

She nodded against his chest. "Asleep. I thought I was supposed to be the smart one. You're going to tell me that since I am asleep, this has to be real. If I thought I was awake, I'd truly be dreaming."

"Something like that. I have help on this side, but I have a mission for you." He pulled away from her embrace and drew the baron Samedi's veve with the ketchup squirt bottle. "Show this image to Delphine de Galpion. There's a loa of the dead, Maman Brigitte, who will be on the lookout for you. With their help, figure out the locations of the gates of Guinee and in what order they're to be entered, and then place the offerings on the correct tombs at the correct times. I know that's a lot to ask, but if we can unite the six other loas of the dead, they can end Malveaux's possession of my body."

She traced the symbol with her fingers. "I've had some thoughts as well about freeing you, but as he's sharing your body, maybe it'd be best to keep them secret. When do you want to start?"

"Easter Sunday is in two weeks. Do you think you could be ready in time?"

She bit her lip, an indication she was running a mental calculation. "We'd want to end on Easter—a celebration of rebirth—as we bring you back. I'll make it work. Can you hang in there for another two weeks?"

"Just knowing salvation is coming will give me strength."

---

*T*he small voodoo library in Scratch and Sniff made Kendell claustrophobic. She'd already spent too much time convulsing, being separated from her body, and frustrated by the unread journals in the dark room. Now she was beginning another adventure that had its roots in the humid room filled with the stench of too many incantations.

She pulled out her drawing of the baron Samedi's veve. "Are you familiar with this cross?"

She no longer saw Delphine as the powerful voodoo priestess. The woman had skills and knowledge, but her limitations had become stumbling blocks.

"Of course. Legend is it's a map of the seven gates, but no one has been able to decipher it fully."

"I know someone who can, but only together can we find her."

Delphine leaned back in her ornately carved wooden chair. "Then what?"

"I had a visit from Myles. He's enlisted the help of Papa Ghede. If we can open the seven gates, we can send Archibald Malveaux to the afterlife where he belongs."

Delphine picked up the piece of paper and looked at it like it was some tourist flyer advertising a nighttime haunted walk through a cemetery. "You think you're the first to try and open the seven gates? Even Marie only got as far as identifying the seven loas of the dead who guard the entrances to Guinee. If you're wrong in any of your calculations, you risk letting the dead back into the world of the living or being dragged through the gate yourself. Were that to happen, the baron Malveaux would be the least of your worries."

Kendell didn't miss that Delphine had said *you* instead of *we*. "That's where Maman Brigitte comes in. She'll help make sure we get it right."

Delphine slid the paper back across the table. "I know I bear responsibility for your boyfriend being possessed by Baron Malveaux, and I'll do what I can to free him. What you're asking, though, is too dangerous. To save one person, you would risk tearing open the fabric of reality that separates us from a living hell."

As a rational woman, Kendell had discounted zombies, ghosts, and witches as horror-story entertainment. Then her concept of ghosts was challenged when Myles had taken her into the realm of spirits. Witchcraft closely paralleled what she'd learned from Delphine. And with the latest challenge, she was forced to accept that even zombies weren't just the work of fiction.

"Thanks to us, the baron Malveaux has already opened that gate," Kendell said. "Even though he's the first one to pass through, there's no reason to hope he'll be the only one. Should it suit his needs to have company, who knows who else he might invite to join him."

Delphine stared at her for longer than Kendell thought necessary. "I'll bet Myles doesn't win many arguments against you." She drew another veve next to the baron Samedi's. "This is the symbol for Maman Brigitte. If she is expecting us, perhaps it will serve as the token to get us to her. I'm not promising my help, but meeting her would be the first step."

Leaving the land of the living to communicate with the powers that watched over the dead wasn't a process that got any easier. Without Myles's steady guidance, Delphine's poor imitation of his skills was like riding in a car being driven by a toddler who couldn't operate the pedals and steering wheel at the same time. Kendell would have been glad to close her eyes to the chaos that circled her, but being pure spirit made the physical action meaningless. The whirlwind finally died down but not before she'd lost her lunch far away in the land of the living.

Her first thought on seeing the emerald-eyed strawberry blonde decked out in a stylish professional skirt and jacket worthy of a lawyer was they'd made the spiritual version of dialing the wrong number. "I'm sorry to bother you."

The woman's heavily Scottish brogue didn't change that impression. "You're Kendell. I've been expecting you."

"I don't understand. I was supposed to be meeting a voodoo loa of the dead. Who are you?"

"Those of the voodoo persuasion call me Maman Brigitte. I'm proud to say I'm the only Caucasian loa of the dead, wife to Baron Samedi."

Kendell turned to Delphine, but the voodoo priestess appeared as only a wavering shadow.

"I allowed your friend here only as a means of your transport. She can listen in but not participate."

Kendell nodded her acceptance. "You're familiar with why I need your help?"

"The imposter, Baron Malveaux, has possessed your spiritual mate."

The revelation nearly shocked Kendell out of her state. She and Myles had only just begun their relationship. Having someone from the spirit realm declare them soul mates left her both warmed to the core and terrified, but she didn't have time for such concerns. "Delphine de Galpion is worried my quest will open the door between the living and the dead."

"That's why you need me. Think of me as your attorney. I'll represent you in Guinee. As you open each gate, I will be standing there to keep you from being taken into the afterlife."

Being sucked through that gate was a concern but only a personal one. Letting loose the zombie apocalypse was a much bigger danger. "What about those among the dead who'd like to return to the land of the living?"

"I am only a moderator, not a guardian. My job isn't to ferry those who have died to the other side. That is the purview of the Ghede barons. But I rule the cemeteries. No one escapes once I've passed judgment."

"And you will ensure that the spirit of Archibald Malveaux returns to the dead?"

The woman crossed her freckled pale-white arms over her silk blouse. "That I cannot do. He is close enough to being a Ghede that my powers over him are limited. You will need to separate Myles from Malveaux. With the gates open, those of us in Guinee will hold the evil spirit. I will then make sure Myles regains full and sole use of his body."

Kendell suspected that would be the best she could hope for, but there was one other soul she had to consider. "What can be done for my ancestor, Lilianna Broussard? She and six others have been held in Guinee—prevented from crossing into the *deep waters*."

"This is a matter for the Ghede family. The women have been used as bribes. We will judge our own."

Kendell knew the risks, and hearing that Maman Brigitte wasn't all-powerful hadn't come as a surprise. "Myles is worth the risk, at least to me. Show me how the veves of you and Baron Samedi fit together."

The woman conjured the two symbols, one in each hand, and fit them together as though they were pieces of a three-dimensional puzzle. Cemeteries and crypts appeared out of the chaos of lines. Kendell turned to the wavering shadow of Delphine, who nodded as she studied each image. They had their plan for the seven gates.

∾

KENDELL KNEW what she had to do—study. Madam Delphine de Galpion wasn't a huckster, but her skills were not even close to what was needed to free Myles. The one thing the voodoo woman did have was a library. Even before Cheesecake had become Kendell's soul puppy, books had been old friends. The answer of how to separate Myles from the baron Malveaux had to be somewhere in that room filled with long-unread incantations. Like any good librarian, Delphine was only too happy to have her precious charges revered and used for their intended purposes. It took only moderate convincing to gain unrestricted access, even when she wasn't present.

Each day after serving coffee, Kendell rushed across the Quarter to Scratch and Sniff perfumery. Delphine slept until six each afternoon. That gave Kendell five hours of uninterrupted investigation into the old books of curses. The first day of translating the words into English, and then decoding the messages, had been totally frustrating. With the baron's glasses, however, Kendell was able to use the dark power to read the journals easily as if they were children's stories. And like books written for someone still learning the basics, much of what the journals contained was either repetitious, overly simplistic, or downright incorrect.

Kendell took off the glasses and tossed them on her page of notes. Four days of study would have been nothing in college, but with the baron running around in Myles's body, every minute might lead to some unimagined disaster. The possibilities filled her nightly dreams.

"Any luck?" Delphine peered over her shoulder.

"What do you know about musical incantations?"

The dark woman took her customary seat across from Kendell, but now she was the student, and Kendell felt like a teacher struggling to stay one class session ahead. "Like smell, music is an underappreciated gateway into the hidden reaches of the soul."

Kendell considered giving her a failing grade for the answer. Delphine had a general knowledge of most of what was hidden in her library but hadn't bothered to delve below the obvious. "For tomorrow, I'd like a list of curses Marie cast using song—though, as the only cursed item I've got left is those glasses, I don't see how I can get the band to play a number worthy of breaking the possession."

"The curse will only hinder what you want to do. The baron Samedi will detect the dark energy. Remember, Marie's original curse wasn't intended to harm Archibald Malveaux, only his heirs."

Just perfect. At least the limitation meant she wouldn't be getting stink eye from Cheesecake. "Myles always said I played better without the curse's amplification."

Delphine pulled a rough-hewn wooden crate out of her bag. Opening the box, she revealed a hideous wood sculpture that resembled a tormented man. "This was left by Marie Laveau. She received it from a freed slave from West Africa. Think of it as part voodoo doll, part spirit jar, and part ancestral totem. The blue-glass jar in its belly will be able to contain the baron Malveaux's spirit. Should Maman Brigitte fail to find a loa of the dead capable of transporting Malveaux to the *deep waters*, this totem might be our only hope for containing him."

Just looking at it gave Kendell the creeps. Square-cut nails had been hammered into its head, though she couldn't tell if they were meant to imitate hair or instruments of torture. "We still need to figure out how to separate Myles from the baron."

"There's a dance of the loa called the banda. It will attract the dark spirits, including the baron Malveaux's. I'll warn you, the dance is considered one of the most sexually explicit ever conceived. The loas pride themselves on their sexual perversions. If we can convince the spirits of the seven women to dance, Malveaux might be tempted out by their flirtations."

Kendell imagined that women dancing naked around a bonfire would be required at some point. Hopefully, the musicians would be exempt from the dress-less code. "I have some ideas regarding musical pieces that might work as accompaniment."

～

KENDELL KNEW Myles would have a hissy fit if he knew about her wandering past the Central Business District to a spot under the freeway overpass at night. The area was a good place for an attractive young woman to meet with an unfortunate end, but she had to test Whit's promise, and this was the most likely spot to find the person she needed.

As she approached Camp Street, she knew she wasn't alone. The shuffling sound of soft soles against the cement sidewalk was too close for comfort.

You'd better be right. She stopped and turned to the man following her. "I'm Kendell Summer."

"I know. Even angels sometimes need protection. You wouldn't be down here among the homeless unless you needed something from us. Just name it."

She breathed a little easier. Thinking of herself as safe among the indigent didn't come easily after a lifetime of being told to be wary. "I need to keep tabs on Myles Garrison's location. He's dressed like a rich old-time banker. Most days, he's at the New Orleans Bank and Trust, but I need to know where he is at all times. Can you help?"

"He's been seen quite often with Abigail Laroque. Don't look so surprised. We don't just keep our eyes on ordinary people. You think we wouldn't know the names of the rich and powerful?"

She might be the daughter of their patron saint, but that didn't mean she was immune to their sarcasm. "I'm going to need to have him abducted. It'll have to be a covert mission to keep the police from ruining everything I have planned."

The man rubbed his bristle-covered chin. "He doesn't frequently wander into our neighborhoods. But he has shown a marked interest in some of the seedier strip clubs. Give me a couple of days, and I should be able to convince some friends of friends to entice him into our clutches."

She reminded herself that it was the baron Malveaux who was seeking out sexual pleasures and not Myles. "I need him on Easter Sunday by late afternoon. If you know me, then you know my people across the river. That's where I need him delivered."

"We will do what we can. Now, if you'll allow me, I'll

escort you out of this area. Those of us who are longtime residents under the overpass know who you are, but that doesn't mean you have universal safe passage down here. There are always strangers around."

She didn't ask his name. It wasn't a matter of not wanting to know. He was one of many. To focus her request on only him would be an insult to the others and an undue burden on the individual. Instead, she reached out and took his hand. "Thank you."

He walked her to the edge of the Quarter. "You'll be safe from here."

She agreed, and having him continue with her would only attract the attention of the police anyway. "I suspect you know where I live. If there's a problem, find me."

"We'll let your family know to expect you."

He turned down an alleyway. Though she could still make him out among the dumpsters, she knew he was as unnoticeable as the street's potholes to everyone else.

Her next stop wasn't as seedy, but the dudes were less classy. Without Myles to provide cover for her presence in the bar, she was just another woman to be hit on by the inebriated assholes who didn't know how to accept a woman's brush-off.

It took an uncomfortably long five minutes to get the bartender's attention. "Hey, Charlie. I need a favor. It's for Myles. Can you lay your hands on a high-quality, historic-brand bottle of rum?"

Charlie poured a drink for the letch who had slid onto the seat next to her but spun it far enough down the bar that the man had to get up to fetch it like a stray dog after a bone. "Anything to entice him back to work. Are we talking sipping rum or fancy cocktails?"

She leaned in to avoid being overheard. "We're talking an offering to the loas of the dead."

His eyes didn't leave hers as he favored her with a laugh at the assumed joke. "Myles said you had a bit of a sexy-witch vibe about you. Hang on for a bit, and I'll dig you up something from the back room." Before he left, he motioned to a shot girl in an unbelievably short black dress. "Keep an eye on my friend. She's Myles's girlfriend. It wouldn't do if she got swept away by one of our dashing customers while I wasn't looking."

"I'll distract anyone who might get too frisky." The girl gave Kendell a wink as she twirled the rack of colorful test tubes filled with alcohol.

Kendell wasn't sure she needed the help, but the men did turn their heads toward the flirtatious bar girl instead of making eye contact.

Charlie returned with a paper bag to disguise his treasure. "Mount Gay Rum, one of the oldest distillers in the world. This bottle of 1703 is one of only twelve thousand released this year. It's made in Barbados. This should please pirate captain and voodoo king alike."

She was afraid to ask. "What do I owe you?"

"You think I'd let Myles Garrison's girlfriend pay for a drink? I'll settle up with him when the time comes. I like the thought of him owing me a favor."

22

"*D*o we have to do this at night?" Saint Louis Cemetery No. 1 was creepy enough during the day. Lit by only the full moon, the aboveground tombs left Kendell wondering how many spirits were about to mug her.

Delphine pulled a set of keys from her satchel. "During the day, tour groups fill the cemetery. The guards are pretty careful about preventing vandalism, which includes not letting people make offerings to the dead."

"And how is it that you have access at night?"

Despite Delphine's dark features, Kendell could make out her look of consternation in the dim light.

"Families of the dead are allowed in at any time." The voodoo priestess pointed toward a crypt. "That's the resting place of Marie Laveau. Once I proved my identity to the authorities, they were only too happy to grant access to an actual descendent of the voodoo queen."

"So how does this work? We leave a shot of rum inside the cemetery gate and leave?"

Delphine swung the gate closed and locked it behind her. "Unfortunately, no. Each gate of Guinee corresponds to an individual tomb. We're in luck with our first mission as it's Marie's tomb. It'll get more complicated after tonight."

"What happens after we leave our offering?"

"I don't know. Maybe nothing. No one who knows what they're doing has ever tried opening the gates."

The brick-and-plaster structure didn't look all that different from any of its neighbors. Discrete sets of three Xs were scratched into the fresh white paint. Delphine mumbled an incantation in French and set out the shot glass.

Kendell carefully filled the glass with the rum Charlie had given her. "Is that it?"

"Not quite." The deep, masculine voice caused Kendell to spin around and face a man wearing a dusty, worn tuxedo with long coattails.

Delphine bowed to the man. "You must be Baron LaCroix."

"That I am." He lifted the shot glass and drained it in one gulp. "Join me for a second drink. I would like to hear why such a beautiful young woman would wish the return of a single man or why he would desire to turn away from the *deep waters*. Surely she could find plenty of others willing to share her bed."

Kendell had heard enough from Delphine to know the loa lacked discretion, especially when it came to sex. She took the offered shot glass, poured herself a drink, and did her best to down it as fast as the baron had done with his. "He's a good lay."

The dark man leaned back and let out a laugh that filled the cemetery. "That is a reason to return from the dead. Sex is only truly enjoyable when life and death are at stake."

She handed the glass to Delphine. "Without sex, the afterlife sounds rather dreary."

"Perhaps that's why people don't prefer to stay in Guinee. Seven days without sex is as long as most people can handle. Your poor boy is going on three weeks. You two should have quite the reunion. You have answered well, Kendell Summer. I pledge you my assistance." With that, the loa of the dead faded from sight, but he didn't leave them alone.

A shadow continued to waver against Marie Laveau's tomb. Kendell knew in her heart it was Myles. "I'll bring you back. Stay strong. One more week, and we can embrace again."

Before he could materialize, Delphine took her hand. "We have to leave. Now. You can't stand there tempting him to cross into the land of the living. He'd be no more than a disembodied spirit—a ghost who's lost his way. And he could lead others to cross over as well."

Kendell had to run to keep up with Delphine. "I thought Mother Brigitte was supposed to prevent that from happening."

"Even she can't stop a ghostly invasion. And don't forget, my ancestor lies in the ground here. We don't want to overstay our welcome."

TIME HAD LOST its meaning for Myles. Without needing sleep or food to rejuvenate his body, he'd lost the basic activities that defined each day. The baron Malveaux's actions didn't interest him. Meetings, arguments, shopping for expensive clothing, and frequenting the brothels that Myles didn't know still existed made him sick. He was better off in Guinee. The *deep waters* would have been even better, but he didn't trust himself to return to Kendell once he'd lost himself to all of human consciousness.

Not that the loas of the dead were bad company—far from it. In many ways, they reminded him of Charlie—loud, boisterous, crude in their sense of humor, and always preoccupied with sex. The last attribute made him remember his pubescent years. No one was as fascinated with sex as someone not getting any.

Of all the loas, Ghede Nibo took the most interest in Myles's plight. The handsome young man still displayed knife wounds under the tattered rags of his purple silk shirt. "I will miss you when you leave, Myles Garrison. Where else shall I find such a fetching specimen of human masculinity?"

Though the spirit was often flirtatious, Myles knew him to be one of the most honorable of the loa. "I need to get back to my life—to my people. Being in this in-between dimension pulls at my spirit."

"Doesn't it just? Had it not been for Samedi and Brigitte taking me into their family after death, I would have lost my way. A violent death is such an abomination. Life must be lived to the fullest and only concluded when the spirit has tasted all there is to experience. Promise me on your return to life that you won't turn down a single opportunity to try new things. There's so much I wish I'd done, but regrets are for the living, not the dead. What use are emotions that can't be fulfilled?"

Myles suspected that being neither living nor truly dead, Nibo longed for that which he could no longer embrace. "You've taught me a lot about life. I won't forget."

"Then it is time." He turned toward a dark, desolate cemetery filled with grandiose Greek Revival mausoleums. "Oh, to be as lovely as that girl who longs for your return."

As though passing through an invisible wall, Nibo stepped from the land of the spirit into what the living knew as reality. Myles could only watch as the debonair dandy bowed to Kendell and accepted her offering. Again, he longed to cross over and be with Kendell, even if only as a guardian spirit. He pressed himself to the barrier between the living and the dead, wishing desperately that she could see him.

A woman's hand rested on his shoulder. "You must let her save you. I know it's not in the nature of men to let women come to their rescue, but for the relationship you seek—one of equals—this must be the way."

He turned from his love to look in the emerald-green eyes of the Scottish lass. "Has that worked for you?"

"You do not know my husband, only the imposter who presumes to carry his name. I would never join with someone so disrespectful of humanity's softer half. Male and female do not equal dominant and submissive."

He wondered how much of her heritage she'd retained and how much of what she knew was learned in the afterlife. "Do you remember your life?"

"It was a very different time. Living so close to the land and being in tune with nature required a bond between husband and wife that's hard to explain to those not accustomed to a simpler existence. What your baron Malveaux believes about women—that we are little more than property to be stolen and abused—is only possible for those of great wealth and no morals."

Myles turned back to the scene taking place in the cemetery. "So you recommend the partnership aspect or the relationship I have with Kendell over being her white knight forever riding to her rescue?"

"There is nothing wrong with chivalry, but you must allow her to return the favor and not always be the damsel in distress. Such a dynamic grows tiresome for both parties."

The meetings between the living and the dead took on a kaleidoscopic feel for Myles, each encounter like the last but with minor changes. Every time a loa passed him to meet with Kendell, he feared she would inadvertently do something to annoy the fickle spirits, but with Maman Brigitte encouraging cooperation from the grave and Madam Delphine de Galpion at Kendell's side, he began to believe their plan just might work.

He hoped she'd come prepared as she approached the sixth gate. Even among the loa, Baron Kriminel was mistrusted. Perhaps it was his name, which sounded so much like the legends of how he'd died—convicted of murder. The way Nibo avoided Kriminel at all costs left Myles to speculate his favorite loa might have been the victim.

The tall dark presence stood beside Myles, waiting his turn at the living. "You would accept the torture of returning to life voluntarily? Isn't it better to continue on to the *deep waters* and peace?"

The loa's question cut to Myles's core. Since his first experiences with psychometry, he'd been tempted to take the final plunge into the depths of humanity's true being. "There are still experiences I'd like to have, revelations about life I'd like to discover, and maybe even a chance to understand who I am and why I exist separate from everyone else."

"Do you believe these life events impart some wisdom to the rest of humanity when you die? Or are you arrogant enough to believe you can change the living for the better?"

He'd never given much thought to what happened to what he'd learned once his brain no longer contained the information. "I've only visited the *deep waters*. When I'm there, what I know of life evaporates like the morning fog off a lake. I've never stayed long enough for the vapor of my life to completely dissipate. As for influencing the living, I've never been much good as a teacher."

"So we can remove education as a reason for returning. Is your wish to return really only for that girl entering the gates?"

He saw her get off the streetcar beyond the iron gate. From his vantage point deep in the cemetery, at the crossroads between the living and the dead, he saw those who had passed on climbing aboard the red trolley as though they hadn't realized they'd died. "She makes my life interesting. If you'd asked me to stay before I knew her, I probably would have accepted. Life is cruel. It's not for the weak of spirit. She gives me strength."

"And other than pursuing your own temporary life education, what do you plan on doing with that strength?"

The traditional answer of combating evil probably wouldn't impress someone named *criminal*. "Experience what life has to offer and help others do likewise. If humanity is to evolve, learning can't be contained in one body. Everyone needs to grow together."

Kendell was pouring the traditional offering of rum. She and Madam de Galpion often brought additional offerings other than the libation, but Myles shied away from the barrier on seeing the live black chicken Delphine pulled from under her coat. Though restrained, the bird made a racket that would wake the dead.

"Your guide has done her homework. Life's suffering culminates in death. Most avoid that reality, hoping to pass calmly in their sleep, but only the ones who fully understand it embrace the suffering. Watch what I do without flinching, and you will have my support."

The sights and sounds of the bird being burned alive sickened Myles, but he remained stationary to witness the event. Opposite him, Kendell did likewise without interfering. Being so close to Baron Kriminel, he could feel the dark loa's glee at the sadistic sacrifice. Never having been one to relish another's pain, Myles hadn't fully considered how violently the living resisted death or how close every being was to that razor's edge that separated the two. As the chicken passed on, Myles saw a pure-white bird fly higher and higher into the sky until it disappeared.

Satiated with the violent act, the loa returned to Myles in the land between the living and the dead.

"Was that really necessary?"

"Do you ask for yourself or your friend? Being among the dead, you can see no spirit is ever lost."

He knew he'd asked on Kendell's behalf. She didn't need to see that level of heartless cruelty. But then, he wasn't supposed to be her protector from life's realities. "You've made your point."

$\mathcal{K}$endell was up well before dawn on Easter morning. She'd successfully opened six of the seven gates, but the final quest left her quivering like a leaf in a hurricane. Breaking into the New Orleans Bank and Trust and searching out the baron Malveaux's old office only to leave a shot glass of rum on his desk seemed insane. And that would just be the beginning of the day's activities.

As she considered the day, she rubbed Cheesecake's back so hard the dog turned and nipped at her hand. "Sorry, girl. I should probably leave you at home, but I've never needed you more than today. Once Delphine and I complete our covert break-in, I'll come back for you."

It wasn't much of a challenge finding something inconspicuous to wear. As she considered the array of black coats in her closet—from cocktail to trench—she realized changing professions to become a bank robber wouldn't require much in the way of a wardrobe adjustment. She pulled out a floor-length leather slicker that she'd bought on a whim. Usually, western wear did nothing for her, but the coat reached the top of her boots and made her feel like a secret agent.

The buzzer to the main door that told her Delphine had arrived only heightened Kendell's anxiety. Meeting the loas of the dead was nothing compared to breaking and entering.

Delphine met her outside the apartment. "Good thing we picked a day when the bank would be empty. How's your homeless contingent? No point in risking a run-in with the law if we don't have the president of the bank in custody."

Kendell hated thinking of Myles's possessor, but Delphine was right. If they didn't have the baron Malveaux, there'd be no point in continuing.

They only had to walk a block before coming on a vagrant seemingly asleep in a doorway. "How's it going?" Kendell asked.

The man pushed the filthy LSU ball cap up from his eyes. "Everything's in order. We won't snag him until he leaves the whorehouse. On his days off, he usually enjoys a late morning. The woman he's with has agreed to help. Whit already has his boat tied up under the dock."

"Tell him not to wait for me. I can find my own way. My family on the Westbank should be ready," Kendell said. Having others involved gave her a feeling of not being alone. Not every plan had to pass through her.

Delphine took her arm and directed her toward Royal Street. "We don't have much time. Since we're not stealing anything, I don't think we'll be discovered once we leave, but we've still got to get in and get out undetected."

"Have you had any thoughts on how we might accomplish that?" Kendell had been preoccupied with having to approach the guardians of the dead, and breaking into a bank had been the least of her considerations.

"I've conjured a plan. I just hope the little twerp shows up."

It didn't take long to slink through the shadows and traverse the handful of blocks between her apartment and the imposing institution. Though they had no need for secrecy on the way to the caper, Kendell again felt like an international spy as they avoided anyone who might recognize them.

Delphine directed her to a dimly lit entrance at the side. "Wait here. If this doesn't work, it'd be better if you weren't caught on camera." The dark-skinned woman in the black pantsuit melded so well with the shadows she appeared to pop out of nowhere when she stepped up to the door. Instead of trying to remain unobtrusive, she stared right into the overhead security camera.

To Kendell's shock, the door opened as if she'd been expected. Delphine gave her a quick wave to come along. Sneaking in the doorway, they were confronted by a towering security guard. He stood like a statue as Delphine closed the door.

"I thought you said he was little."

The frightening figure remained rigid, only his jaw moving as he spoke. "Who are you calling little?"

Delphine bowed to the man. "Forgive me, Papa Ghede,

but your physical stature is well known." She turned back to Kendell. "The guard is being possessed by the oldest of voodoo loas. He's on our side or, more appropriately, Myles's side."

Kendell looked at the cold, emotionless eyes. "Thank you."

"Just don't fail." He lifted his arm and pointed down the corridor like a marionette on strings. "You don't have much time before the interior cameras come back online."

She would have felt more comfortable having the guard come with them, but by the way the man stood stiff as a board, she doubted the loa could move the body with much speed. By comparison, the baron's possession of Myles had to be more complete than Kendell wanted to imagine.

Delphine didn't waste any time racing down the hallway, up three flights of stairs, and around a corner to the old wooden doorway. The entrance to the office was out of character with the rest of the building. Kendell would have picked it out immediately. "He didn't worry too much about being sly with the gate's location."

"He didn't think he needed to. Papa Ghede is the only spirit strong enough to overcome the security features—for both the living and the dead—that the baron put in place."

Kendell understood what Delphine meant when she pushed against it. Instead of the door opening, the spirits of the seven women Malveaux had imprisoned took shape. Lilianna stepped forward. "You are not allowed in."

"You know we can stop him. The loas of the dead have promised their support. The other six gates are open. All I need is you."

The young woman wavered in the light. "If you fail, it will be we who suffer."

Kendell hadn't considered the ramifications of failure. Myles would be forever lost. "If this doesn't work, I'll offer myself to the baron Malveaux in exchange for letting you pass to the *deep waters*."

Delphine took her arm. "You don't know what you're saying. You'd be trapped forever."

"I'd be with Myles, and I've seen that Cheesecake can cross over. Why is that, anyway? Can all animals see the dead?"

"That's probably a conversation for another time, but I suspect it had to do with her ingesting that pipe tool."

Kendell nodded. It made sense. So long as she had her dog and her love, nothing else mattered, even if they had to live in purgatory. "Is my offer satisfactory, Lilianna?"

"You're expecting me to feel maternal and give you a pass on your proposal. But I won't. If you fail, I'm not staying in this version of hell."

The doors opened as the women faded from sight.

Delphine pulled out the paper bag. "We'd better hurry." But unlike with the previous gates, she simply poured the shot and left it on the desk.

"Aren't you supposed to do an incantation? Where's the loa?"

Delphine shook her head. "The glass will stay just as it is until the ceremony tonight. I don't want baron Malveaux knowing what we're up to just yet. We don't want him rushing in, or worse, materializing before we're ready. If everything works as planned, the original baron Samedi will show up to collect his tribute. But now we've gotta run."

With every hurried step down the hallways and staircases, Kendell thought for sure they were about to be discovered. As they passed the stationary guard, she saw in his eyes a glimmer of alarm at the intrusion.

She rushed through the door, thinking she'd never been so happy to be out of a building.

"Now, what are you two doing sneaking out of the bank?" The sight of the police lieutenant nearly stopped Kendell's heart.

Slowly, she made out the features of his face in the dark. "Lieutenant Cazenave, it's not what it looks like. We didn't steal anything."

"I'm sure you didn't. The bank's cameras transmit directly to the police station. I thought you might need a little assistance. But before I cover for you again, mind telling me what that excursion was all about?"

All Kendell wanted to do was run as far from the bank as possible. "This really isn't the time or place."

He looked Delphine up and down. She was wearing a skintight leotard. "I suppose not," he said. "I'll expect a full report when this is over."

The way Delphine lowered her head left Kendell to assume the two were more than casual acquaintances. *Just once, I wish people would tell me the whole truth.* She knew she'd only be able to completely trust Myles and no one else.

As they left the lieutenant, Delphine held Kendell's arm to prevent her from breaking into an all-out sprint toward her apartment. "Just because Joe intercepted the video feed, that doesn't mean no one else is watching. We're just two friends out for a Sunday morning stroll after our gym workout."

They each had a lot of work to do, and the first rays of dawn were already lighting the sky. "What's your relationship to the paranormal division of the police department?" She didn't see any point in being diplomatic. If they were about to get sucked into a hell mouth, she'd like to know who was leading the way.

"I supply them with information on what's happening and answer questions about past curses. It's better to have them as a partner than an adversary."

Better for whom? But as with all things related to Delphine, Kendell knew the answer without asking. The woman would do whatever it took to secure her place in the family legend. "Will Lieutenant Cazenave be able to hide our activities?"

"It's Easter Sunday. I doubt there are many police in the station this early. He's always managed to keep me out of jail up to this point."

Again, everything hinged on their success. If they couldn't remove the baron from Myles, no amount of help from outside the Laroque family was likely to free them. Kidnapping a rich and powerful man wasn't the kind of thing to go unpunished.

THE MORNING PASSED in a whirlwind of activity: checking in

on Polly and the band to make sure the equipment was ready, arranging for a delivery of firewood, and picking up her acoustic guitar and Cheesecake for the ferry ride to the Westbank. Even with all the chores, Kendell still made it to the enclave nestled in the cottonwood grove before Whit delivered Myles. She noticed his boat wasn't at the shore. *The baron must have had a wild night. Good. It will be his last.*

Unfortunately, Delphine hadn't made it yet either. There were still six hours until sunset, plenty of time, but Kendell felt insecure without all of the people she needed already surrounding her.

"Not much of a crowd." Polly was keeping active, setting up the equipment on a series of pallets the tribe had scavenged from the river.

"I only need an audience of one, but he's not exactly going to be enthusiastic about the performance."

Polly shrugged. "This is your gig. Lord knows you've done enough for us. We owe you. If you want to put on a private concert, we're with you all the way."

"By sunset, the bonfire should be roaring, the rum flowing, and our audience in his seat. The small village here doesn't have much, but what they can't get for you I'll find a way to scrounge up."

Mary was the next to grab Kendell's attention. "Hawk and some of his friends are hauling the wood over from across the levee. I've got a big pot of gumbo stewing. Anything else we can do?"

Kendell looked upriver at the roofs of the middle-class neighborhood. "They aren't going to bother us, are they?" The last thing she needed was the local police, or neighborhood association, shutting them down for not having a permit.

"I'm more concerned with them trying to join in. We've run a couple of test fires earlier this week. At first, it was just the drunks from the bar who stumbled over, but last night, we had a group of kids who wanted to use the place as a make-out spot."

She hadn't considered the dangers of their activity being seen by the public. "I'd like to limit how many people join in, but I guess with the music, that's going to be pretty difficult."

"Honey, I don't mean to butt into your business, but family is family, and legend is legend. Whit dropped off a bag of special herbs he procured downriver. We thought if things got a little... unexplainable, we might toss the weeds in the fire. Once our unwanted visitors breathe in the smoke, their mental confusion might make a good cover for anything they weren't meant to see."

Kendell gave Mary a good hard hug. "Maybe you should go ahead and add it at the start."

Mary looked around at her family. "You don't need to worry about us. Considering what most of us drink, eat, and smoke, we don't put much stock in what we see and hear. Whit says the guy he's escorting across the river might not be too willing. I prepared a special blend of my private stash to ease his apprehensions."

Giving Myles pot, or some hallucinogen, hadn't been part of the plan, but Kendell knew enough other religions believed in the transformative nature of drugs that she shouldn't discount the idea. After all, Delphine made something of a specialty out of her blends of scents. Based on some of their sessions together, Kendell had to assume not all of them were benign. "When Delphine gets here, let her have a smell of what you've prepared. I think you two might find you have a lot in common. Are you sure no cop is going to bust up our gathering?"

"It's our land. I filed the deed you gave me at the courthouse. It's a clusterfuck of a case, but we do have a lawyer working for us pro bono. I don't know how it will end. For now, however, we've got legal use of this little slice of heaven secured for us by our angel."

Cheesecake raced around Kendell's feet like a one-year-old puppy and headed out toward the river. Three children were in hot pursuit. Kendell was grateful for the distraction. "She hasn't played like that in years." But her enjoyment at watching her pup was short-lived.

Out on the Mississippi, Whit's small battered wooden skiff struggled through the current. It wasn't the waves, however, that were causing the boat's rocking. Between Delphine at the front, guiding, and Whit at the back, piloting, lay a tied-up bundle that thrashed from side to side. Kendell's relief at seeing they'd secured Myles was overshadowed by fear that the baron who inhabited his body might dump him overboard in his rage.

Polly nudged Kendell. "I hope that's not our guest. He looks pissed. Your plan may not be the best introduction of a music producer to our sound."

"I hate to disappoint you, but today really isn't about furthering the band's reputation." Kendell knew the time had come. She wouldn't be able to keep his identity a secret.

"It's Myles. He's suffering what could be described as a dual identity. I'm hoping to bring him back to reality."

"Do you really think I'm that conservative? I know a possession when I hear one. With all your little magical objects and how they affect our playing, I'd have to be pretty dense to ignore the source of your power. What's the plan, witchy woman?"

It wasn't that Kendell didn't trust Polly with the truth, but some reality-stretching ideas weren't easy to explain. "It's a long story, and I don't come off looking too good in how Myles ended up in his predicament. I have to save him. Explaining what's going to happen today, or at least what I hope happens, would sound crazy. All I can say is, prepare for a wild ride."

"Those are the best kinds of gigs." Polly left to finish up the musical preparations.

Once the boat hit shore, Cheesecake changed from the fun-loving puppy to the wolf-protector. Kendell had to sprint to snatch up the dog before she had a chance to jump into the skiff and maul the demon bagged and tied in the center of the boat. "Stop, girl. It's Myles. I know it doesn't seem like him, but you have to trust me." She turned to Delphine. "Pull the cover off his face. Cheesecake needs to see him so she'll calm down."

But seeing the face so distorted in anger didn't help either Cheesecake or Kendell. "You meddlesome little girl. You'll pay for this—you and everyone around you. Kill me, and I'll just possess someone else. You'd be doing me a favor. I can't believe I got stuck in this weak-willed, powerless man-child."

His words struck fear in her heart but not because of his threats. She'd been manipulated into bringing the baron Malveaux back from the dead, but whoever was pulling the strings also limited what the baron could do. Simply opening the gates would have given him power to possess whomever he pleased. By focusing that energy into one person, Kendell, who had deposited it in someone else, Myles, they'd locked Malveaux into one body with all of its limitations.

"I brought you into this reality," she said, "and I'm going to force you out."

His sneer, coming from Myles's mouth, left her glad her boyfriend didn't have that evil streak in his soul. "Do your worst. When this little festival of yours is over, I'll have control of you all."

Delphine returning the gag to his mouth prevented the baron's vitriol from spilling out to the gathering. Unfortunately, from his vantage point as host to the bastard, Myles wasn't able to as easily shut him up. *"Your girlfriend has no idea what she's in for. Once I'm free of you, I'm going to possess her body and offer it to every brothel I find."*

Myles had lost his ability to be shocked by anything the baron said. *"You realize it would be you being fucked, right? I mean, it's not like I've paid any attention to what you've been up to these last few weeks."*

"Shut up! You can't tell me you weren't watching while I spent my nights with sweet young women. She'll know what I'm doing

to her. *And once I've wrung that youthful purity from her, I'll possess some guy who will finish the job on her. You'll be powerless to stop me. The two of you should have left that dog to her fate and never gotten involved."*

Threatening Kendell was one thing—she could fend for herself—but Myles thought saving Cheesecake might have been the noblest thing he'd ever done in his life. *"You really don't know anything about love at all, do you?"* But before the baron could continue the argument, Myles felt a constriction in his throat. Though unpleasant, it was the first physical sensation he'd had since his body had been confiscated. "What's going on?"

"Shut up." The baron's animosity was noticeably tempered by a sense of calm.

Though Myles had an extensive understanding of all of the various alcohols served at the bar, he avoided other intoxicants. But any halfway social college graduate knew the smell of pot if not completely its effects. The aroma, mixed with other herbs and burlap, reminded him of Madam de Galpion's comments about smell being a powerful reminder of past memories. The baron's hold over his senses couldn't compete with the soothing cannabis. Unfortunately, all Myles was able to see with his renewed sight was the bag over his head and the smoke that was filtering in through the loose weave.

"At least he's calming down." The sound of Kendell's voice made him wish he could tell her whatever she was doing was working, but the baron still had control of his physical actions.

"It's nearly twilight—time we lit the bonfire. Is your

band ready?" Madam de Galpion's voice wasn't as welcome, but Myles knew Kendell would need help to free him. He just hoped she wasn't about to release something even worse.

"We'll be in full swing by the time the fire's raging."

The effect of the drugs made it hard to know if the chanting he was hearing was from Polly Urethane and the Strippers or some ancient Celtic cult. One voice rose above the rest, much to the baron's consternation. *"They brought that fucking witch back to haunt me?"*

From the baron's reaction, Myles knew the singer was Maman Brigitte. Her voice, however, wasn't in the land of the dead where he'd met her. With Polly Urethane and the Strippers providing accompaniment, she was singing through an outdoor sound system.

The song took on a harder edge reminiscent of the music he'd heard at the Scratchy Dog. It made his heart beat faster—his heart, no longer controlled by the baron. As Maman Brigitte's voice moved from the stage to the crackling fire, someone took the sack off his head.

Madam de Galpion stared hard into his eyes. "It's working. But we've still got a fight ahead of us. Time to try and separate the two beings."

The baron still had control of Myles's muscles. Instead of turning to the stage to look for Kendell, he watched the disembodied spirit of the Scottish voodoo loa as it moved toward the bonfire. His heart beat harder, but this time, it was the baron reacting. *My women.*

Myles couldn't immediately see what had attracted his attention. As the fire leapt into the sky, he noticed that not all of the visual distortions were from the flames. The spirits of seven naked women danced with wanton abandon in and around the burning logs. Standing in front of them all, singing like a Siren enticing Odysseus from his home, was Maman Brigitte, and the baron was helpless to resist her.

The baron Malveaux continued to focus on the fire and began to lose the strength that kept Myles imprisoned. Myles was able to turn his head toward the angelic acoustic-guitar sound coming from the stage. He made eye contact with his lovely Kendell. The band softly accompanied her.

"'Gimme a Man after Midnight'? ABBA again? Really?" His voice came out raspy. But her sweet singing, combined with the inside joke, forced a laugh from his throat.

Sitting nearby, Madam de Galpion began a voodoo incantation. The sound sent the baron into a blind rage. "Your spells won't work on me! You think I'm so naïve as to be drawn through the seventh gates by such obvious trickery?"

The voodoo priestess appeared not to notice the outburst as she continued her chant.

"Don't be alarmed, but I'm here with you." Though Kendell still sang on stage, she was also next to him in the spirit world.

"How?" he asked.

"I've always told you music is transformative for me."

The philosophical discussion would have to wait. *"What's next?"*

Her heart melded with his. *"Battle."*

Turning back to the baron, he saw the women's spirits

pulling at their captor. Simply being freed, however, wouldn't prevent the baron from repossessing him. Myles had to defeat the powerful spirit on his own.

As if hearing his thoughts, Madam de Galpion released his physical restraints. Like a drunk at an orgy, he joined the women around the bonfire in a dancing, lusty struggle for control. The intoxicants, both physical and magical, leveled the spiritual playing field, and the baron was the outsider.

Myles considered violence simply the physical manifestation of intense outrage. Deprived of using his fists, he focused on his fury. "This is my body—my life. You are nothing more than a parasite with delusions of power. Leave me, and return to the realm of the dead."

Though the baron had only made strong arguments while in charge, now that he didn't have complete control, he resorted to violence. Myles grew dizzy as his body swung around as though trapped in a whirlwind. *"I am the baron Malveaux, true incarnation of the baron Samedi. Your body, and all those around me, are my possessions. You are merely the tenants."*

"Even tenants have a right to privacy." Instead of delving into the world of human consciousness, Myles drew forth all the power his soul could contain and released the lightning bolt of indignation directly at the baron.

The seven spirits of the women the baron had wronged pulled at him like harpies from hell. Myles felt his angel, Kendell, doing the same to him. The unwanted union split, but rather than relief, Myles thought an appendage was being ripped from the socket of his soul.

From behind Kendell's spirit, a wolf the size of a bear

lunged toward the half-severed and mangled energy of his spirit. But the attack wasn't aimed at Myles. The baron released his final hold, which had been sucking Myles dry, and shot out of his body. Like a sheepherder directing a border collie, Madam de Galpion used her canting to direct the wolf to cut off the baron's attempt to join his women. Without a body, the baron's clawing at the ground proved useless, and his energy was whisked into the wooden voodoo doll at the priestess's feet.

Finally freed of the demon spirit, Myles collapsed in front of the fire. The wolf returned to Cheesecake's body and came running up to kiss his forehead even before Kendell laid down her guitar and rushed from the stage. The last thing he felt before passing out was her cradling his head in her lap while Cheesecake sniffed him all over to make sure none of the baron remained.

$\mathcal{M}$yles woke to the smell of coffee, bacon, and eggs. He'd never been one for big breakfasts, but the homey aromas made him snuggle down deeper under the billowy comforter, anticipating a long, lazy morning. After weeks of being denied his senses, he relished every smell, taste, sight, and sound—especially those of Kendell and Cheesecake as they puttered around the apartment.

Kendell came in wearing his T-shirt and carrying a breakfast tray, with Cheesecake at her feet. "I hoped the smell of my cooking might wake you up from the dead. You've been conked out for fourteen hours."

It felt like it had been much longer as he tried to force his achy body to sit up. "It was good to sleep again. I don't know how to describe the state between the living and the dead, under the baron's control, but it wasn't restful."

"He's gone now." She snuggled next to him and pulled

Cheesecake up with her. "We can lie in bed all day if you want. For the first time in I don't even know how long, there's no crisis threatening to tear at the fabric of reality. At least, not one that demands our attention."

"What happened to the baron? Last I saw, he was being sucked down the drain into some wooden sculpture."

The time she took sipping her coffee made him think he wasn't going to like her answer. "It's all a bit complicated. We couldn't send him back to Guinee, and without going through that portal, we couldn't send him to the *deep waters*. I made a promise to Lilianna that she'd never have to deal with him again. Though we had six of the seven gates open, I couldn't risk him ending up exactly where he started."

"I thought you made offerings to all seven loas."

She scratched Cheesecake's ear, a sure sign that she was looking for support from her pup. "Baron Malveaux wasn't Baron Samedi, but he was standing in the gate and preventing the real baron from doing his job. Delphine thought once we had control of Malveaux, Samedi would make himself known and we could push him along, as it were. But we needed a fallback plan. That was the voodoo fetish totem."

The whole plan began to smell suspicious. "She just *happened* to have a totem handy?"

"I know you don't trust her, but I didn't see a lot of alternatives. She has the totem, with the baron Malveaux locked inside, in her curio cabinet that sits in front of her voodoo library."

He remembered the floor-to-ceiling glass case. "There

were other statues in that display. Please tell me they aren't all imprisoning evil spirits."

"I didn't ask, not that she would have told me or I would have believed her." Kendell leaned her head back against his bare chest. Her black hair smelled of bonfire, lavender, and cannabis from the day before. "All I cared about was getting you back and sending that motherfucker someplace where he couldn't do any more harm. As far as leaving the totem with Delphine is concerned, she said it would complete our payment to her for her services."

He couldn't deny Kendell's vulgarity. "I can't help feeling that we used a Band-Aid on a heart attack."

Her giggle never failed to warm his heart. "It's not that bad. I know it's not as permanent a solution as either of us would have liked, but those who were in danger, both the living and the dead, are now safe."

"And what about Baron Samedi? Now that Malveaux's out of the way, has the offering been accepted?"

She started sipping at her coffee again. "We don't know. The gate was in the New Orleans Bank and Trust. That's not exactly a place we can go check. Even if it was, though, once Delphine put the baron in the totem, we lost the opportunity to send him to hell—or wherever the loas of the dead keep someone like that."

"And his belongings?"

At the rate she was savoring her coffee, he wondered why her cup wasn't already empty. "You mean the curse? I had to turn over the seven objects we modified. That means I have a secret weapon among the Laroques should they want to confront us again. Though with the baron removed and his women's spirits freed, I'm not sure what power remains in the items. Minerva took the rest of the stuff in the four trunks to her garage. I don't imagine anyone will be looking for them. It's just old stuff at this point."

He hoped she was right about the curse no longer having any power, but after what they'd been through, her explanation sounded naïve. "So with any luck, we're done trying to save the world from some mysterious curse. Tell me about the music. I saw you in the spirit realm while you were playing. How did you manage to be two places at the same time?"

With her foot, she petted Cheesecake, who was relaxing in a spot of sun. "I learned that from my girl. Call it astral projection. I think by taking what you taught me and adding in the modification we did to the curse, I ended up with the ability to leave my body without really leaving my body."

He understood the idea of moving between realities—hell, he'd taught her about it. But he'd never been able to set his body on autopilot while he was away. "I don't get it."

"I don't fully understand either. When I was talking to Maman Brigitte, Cheesecake was with me. At first I thought it was because she was lying next to me, but later, I figured it had something to do with her swallowing that pipe tool. Either way, she wasn't freaked out. It almost seemed natural to her to be a spirit wolf by my side. It had to do with our connection."

"Still not getting it." He began to wish there was rum to add to his coffee.

"I've never really been able to explain what I feel when I

play music onstage. I connect to people. Sure, they're out on the dance floor, watching me, but really, I'm the voyeur—and not just because I'm observing their reactions. Often, I'll see one or two people I really connect to. The way they move or sing along or clap is an opening into their souls. I had never pressed the ability before yesterday, but you needed me. My music was what connected us. I had to keep playing, but I also had to be with you. Maybe it was my love for you, or maybe it was all the pot Whit kept tossing on the bonfire. I had a pretty intense contact high for being outside."

He could almost understand. Playing music for her wasn't about logic. She lost herself to the performance, and that had nothing to do with the cursed objects. "I was glad you were there with me. Cheesecake nearly gave me a heart attack as a wolf, though. Not that I didn't know she had it in her, but I was damn glad she wasn't lunging at me. Just make me one promise."

She turned to him with her caring, soulful eyes. "Anything."

"Never again play anything by ABBA for me."

In Minerva's garage, Kendell adjusted her electric guitar for their final rehearsal before the band's next gig. Musicians and addiction were a deadly combination. She had all but promised Myles and Cheesecake that she wouldn't delve back into the dark magic. Their concerned faces would be all she'd need to remember to stay on the wagon.

The band, however, was a different story. Had it only been drugs or alcohol, she could make the argument that going cold turkey would help their performance. As the cursed objects amplified the band's inherent skills, however, convincing each member that they played better untainted was more of a challenge.

"I just don't want to go back to playing for half-empty nightclubs." Predictably, Polly was the hardest to convince.

To Kendell's surprise, however, Scraper was on Kendell's side. "I've done my time with drugs. Cocaine can make you go all night, and you think you've mastered something otherwise unattainable. Playing with your curse felt a lot like that to me. If I can't slap the bass without the enhancement, then I'm not much good as a musician."

Minerva often followed the lead of her partner in the rhythm section. "My muscles didn't get as fatigued with the curse, but the next day, they felt like overstretched rubber bands. I think I've learned what I can under the influence."

"What did you learn?" Kendell hadn't considered that there might have been a lesson under the intense adrenaline-fueled playing.

"Don't hold back. Give every bit of energy to every lick. The next song will take care of itself. I used to plan out a gig. You know, like, ration how much energy I was using. With one of those things around, I had no choice but to lay it all on the line with every muscle movement. I can do that without being under some weird paranormal influence."

Only Lynn seemed not to care. "I use music to get out my aggressions. I already focus all that energy into my fingers. The curse didn't seem to make much of a difference to me, though I did think the rest of you played with more vigor."

Kendell hadn't known her quiet, petite friend to ever express anger. "With the way you play, people must piss you off something awful."

Lynn lowered her head as she giggled. "I like people—most of the time."

"Look, I know we had a fair amount of unexpected success with the power of the curse. But it wasn't us, not really. And the part that was *us* is true with or without the added energy. I know there's a little more stress on us now that people are paying attention, but that's just an added reason to show them what we can do. Let's just rock this gig tonight the way we always did—just to have fun and be bandmates on stage."

Polly was still pouting. "I guess we don't have much of a choice."

It would have been easy to agree with her bandleader, but Kendell didn't want to be seen as the usurper taking over the band with her equivalent of magic dust. "Give me tonight. Let me show you that I can still push the envelope all on my own. If you still don't think we can play better on our own, I'll remain open to finding a way to reincorporate the voodoo into the music, but the decision has to be unanimous."

~

THERE WAS a tension Kendell didn't like as the band set up on the small stage at the Scratchy Dog. She felt the weight of their success resting on her shoulders. Those who arrived early and were starting the night off at the bar expected a high-octane show. If only Myles were pouring the drinks. He could at least moderate their level of intoxication.

Kendell strapped on her black electric guitar. The butterflies in her stomach weren't just from the lack of amplified energy.

Polly gave her a wink before taking the microphone. "We have a little surprise for you tonight. Our lead guitarist, Olympia Stain, has asked to sing. So I'm going to sit back with my tambourine and let her take center stage—this one time."

Kendell took a deep breath to calm her nerves before stepping into the spotlight. "This song has a new meaning for me after the last few weeks." Summoning up the skills that would be inherent in Stevie Nicks and Lindsey Buckingham's proverbial lovechild, she hit the opening notes to "Rhiannon." Kendell belted out, "Your life knows no answer" as if she were screaming the words at her recently imprisoned ancestor.

As the music took hold, the smoke that filled the upper balcony attracted her attention. Smoking wasn't allowed. Though no one else would notice, Kendell saw the seven women who had been kept captive by the baron Malveaux dancing with wild abandon to her music. Their long, elegant dresses floated on the air as if lifted by the lyrics.

Her heart skipped a beat as a tall gentleman in a tuxedo and top hat pressed his way between them. For just an instant, she feared Malveaux had escaped, but the elegant figure was too tall and dignified to be her hated ancestor. He lifted his top hat to reveal his naked skull then bowed so low his forehead touched the floor.

The spirits of the seven women continued their joyful dance as each disappeared behind him as though stepping through a doorway. After they had gone, he stood back up and tossed something high over the heads of the audience.

Kendell was just finishing the song as the small object crossed from the shadows into the light. She snatched the gleaming guitar pick out of the air. Inscribed into the gold finish on one side were the words "With Appreciation and Love" and on the other "Papa Ghede and the Loas of the Dead."

Turning back to the balcony, she saw Maman Brigitte standing next to her husband—each blew her a kiss before joining the freed women. Two large wooden doors closed behind them, sealing off the final gate to Guinee and returning the dead to their natural order.

Kendell held the guitar pick up toward Polly. "I think it's time we rocked this place."

"And I know just the song to do it." The bandleader turned to the rhythm section. "'Black Magic Woman' in honor of our lead guitarist. Let's make Fleetwood Mac's original blues band proud."

From the opening chords, Kendell knew the pick wasn't possessed the way the baron Malveaux's things were, but there was a purer power, one that came from Kendell herself. *I suppose being a voodoo queen is a destiny I can't ignore.*

*W*earing his freshly tailored Armani suit, Lincoln Laroque leaned back in his office chair and put his feet, in their highly polished Ferragamos, on his glass desk. The trappings of wealth and power were only the outward manifestations of his ambition. Looking out the window of his penthouse office at the city—his city—he knew he'd outgrown the petty politics his family had spent generations mastering.

He set the leather box the family had held for generations next to the cheap Nike cardboard box. From one, he pulled the cufflink with its modified curse, and from the other, he pulled its match. The two hadn't been united since the death of their original owner. He fastened them to his dress shirt. The *M*s decorated with skulls would be conversation starters to everyone else, and only the family would recognize them as his claim to power. And where the Laroque family focused, money followed.

The young secretary's voice on the intercom made him momentarily irritated at being disturbed. "She's here."

The annoyance quickly passed. "Send her in."

He remained in his position of repose. Polite greetings didn't extend to those in his employ. "Have you got it?"

Delphine de Galpion pulled the ugly folk-art fetish from her canvas bag and set it on this desk next to his feet. "And your end of the bargain?"

He nodded toward his briefcase as if he couldn't be bothered to open it.

She unlatched the catches and pulled forth the six leather-bound journals. Her face told the story. She believed she'd gotten the better end of the deal. Such confidence often loosened people's tongues once they thought the negotiations had ended. "I knew when you sent me those photocopied pages what you were offering, but nothing compares to holding Marie's journals. These are everything your family has of hers?"

"Of her writings, yes. You're holding secrets that have been kept safe for one hundred and fifty years. Added to what you already have, these should make you the most knowledgeable voodoo practitioner that ever lived, assuming you can make out all the writings."

She nodded toward the antique West African spirit statue. "And what will you do with that?"

"My ancestor is right where I want him. I have no desire to fall under his version of authority."

"So that's just a keepsake?"

He finally stood but not out of respect. Some people needed to be physically shown the door. "We have what we want from each other. I'm sure we'll be in touch." So many of his people who were much smarter than Delphine had spent so much time spent trying to figure out the old voodoo queen's writings that he knew she'd be back with questions sooner rather than later.

"You're a busy man." She held up the journals one last time. "Thanks again for these." Her feigned nonchalance only proved how badly she hid her emotions.

Once the door closed, he returned to his desk and hit the intercom button. "I'm not to be disturbed."

He'd played the game to perfection. His meddling mother still ran the bank, but the demise of her power under the harsh glare of the baron Malveaux had been all too easy to predict. Anyone who'd read the family diaries knew the man would never bow to a woman. If those silly kids hadn't recaptured the old goat, the supposed great and powerful voodoo priestess would have jumped at the chance all on her own. Either way, the voodoo journals would be exactly where he wanted them—out of the hands of his family where someone might figure out his play. In the end, the family's base of power had been brought forth, isolated, and distilled into a form he could control. Both the living and the dead would now be at his beck and call. As for any future potential paranormal meddling, he'd keep an eye on the witchy guitarist. Success often had a way of forgiving the sins of those who had provided a boost. And if helping her band along didn't prove to be enough of a distraction, a little nudge might set up an interesting power play between the educated voodoo practitioner and the girl with innate skills of her own. Power wasn't much fun unless it could be used to manipulate others. Winning only meant it was time to reset the board and find a worthier opponent.

He turned the voodoo doll with its mouth and eyes sown shut toward him. "So, great-great-grandfather, let's try this again—my way this time."

BOOK LIST

Technopia Series:
(writing as Greg Chase)
Creation
Evolution
Damnation
Salvation

The Malveaux Curse Mysteries :
(writing as G.A. Chase)
Dog Days of Voodoo
You, Me, and the Voodoo Queen
Oops, I Voodooed Again (coming soon)

Other Stories
Through the Lens

ABOUT THE AUTHOR

G.A. Chase is the pen name for Greg Chase. He is a science fiction and paranormal author living in New Orleans with his wife, fellow author Deanna Chase, and their two shih tzu dogs. On any given day you can find him behind his computer, people watching in the quarter, or out in his studio creating stories in glass. His glass work can be found at www.chase-designs.com.

gregchaseauthor.com

www.ingramcontent.com/pod-product-compliance
Lightning Source LLC
Chambersburg PA
CBHW020318200626
46814CB00006BA/2307